SOMETHING

Judy Allen has worked [...] in a literary agency. But [...] years she has been a full-time writer, and now has over twenty books – some fiction, some non-fiction – to her name.

A sense of place is very important to her, so the non-fiction work she enjoys most is writing guidebooks: "I like to have two projects on the go at once, so that if I get stuck on one I can turn to the other. There's something very uncertain about writing novels – but I know where I am with a guidebook (literally!)."

Place plays an important part in her fiction as well, and she finds that "more often than not, the setting becomes one of the main characters." She is particularly attracted to seascapes and coastlines, "especially the bleak kind where *Something Rare and Special* is set."

Judy Allen won the prestigious Whitbread Award for her eighth children's novel, *Awaiting Developments* and her first adult novel, *December Flower*, was made into a television film. She lives in Putney.

Also by Judy Allen

Awaiting Developments
The Dream Thing
The Lord of the Dance
Song for Solo and Persistent Chorus
The Spring on the Mountain
The Stones of the Moon
Travelling Hopefully

Something Rare and Special

❋

Judy Allen

WALKER BOOKS
LONDON

First published 1985 by Julia MacRae Books
This edition published 1989 by Walker Books Ltd
87 Vauxhall Walk, London SE11 5HJ

© 1985 Judy Allen
Cover illustration © 1990 Julie Douglas

Reprinted 1990

Printed in Great Britain by Cox and Wyman Ltd, Reading
Typeset in Great Britain by Computape (Pickering) Ltd

British Library Cataloguing in Publication Data
Allan, Judy
Something rare and special.
I. Title
823'.914 [F]
ISBN 0-7445-0846-0

Contents

Chapter One

Somewhere a bird flew, mostly over sea but sometimes passing over the shore. It was a white bird with a deeply forked tail and a red bill. It would have looked quite spectacular on its own, but it was flying with a cloud of identical birds and there was nothing that marked it out from the rest as it fished with them, rested on the sea with them, joined in their noisy squabbles.

Lyn stood outside the big swing doors of the school, pretending to jog gently on the spot but not actually lifting either foot from the imitation cobbles of the school fore-court. It was time to go home, indeed most people already had, but she was still casting about for a legitimate reason to stay around a little longer. It was only partly because she liked school, although she did. It was mostly because there was something she was trying not to think about – something she knew, but wished that she didn't know. At school it was forced to get out of her head to make way for all that was going on. On the way home, though, it would nag to get back in, and by the time she was at home it would be there, taking up all her thought space.

She usually managed to kill a little time with Sue, but Sue had left as soon as school was over today to, as she put it, go and wave her teeth at the dentist. And Leila had had to rush home to see some visiting aunt. Leila, Lyn thought, probably had more aunts than Sue had teeth. And Winston had had to hurry back to have his tea early because his parents were going out. One way and another everyone seemed to have important business to attend to today. And the fact that none of it was anywhere near as important as the thing Lyn was trying not to think about didn't seem to help at all.

I'll give it a count of twenty-five, she thought, beginning to jog on the spot more vigorously so that her feet actually left the ground at each step, and then I'll go home. A few children were still wandering out of the school's double doors – some turning right towards the road and its bus stops, some walking left along the pedestrian precinct to the newspaper-cum-sweet shop.

Six, seven, eight, nine, ten, Lyn counted silently, in time with the rhythm of her feet. The pedestrian precinct, which was like a long arm with the fist of the school at its end, flicked up and down to the same beat, like the picture on a badly tuned television set. Fifteen, sixteen, seventeen, eighteen. At the far end of the precinct – like the main body of the beast whose arm and fist curved out towards her – rose the six mighty towers of the Estate, linked by level upon level of covered walkway, the whole structure dark against the light spring sky, like a giant's castle, an ogre's fortress. Twenty, twenty-one, twenty-two. Out of the doors behind Lyn came the new girl, walking slowly, her head rather down.

"Hallo," said Lyn as she drew level. "What's your name, again?"

The new girl sniffed and muttered something that Lyn couldn't hear – then she raised her head a bit and tried again. "Sharon," she said. Her eyes looked all watery. She had only started at the school that morning, just past the middle of term, and this was the first time Lyn had actually heard her speak, although she supposed she must have given her name to the teacher at some point.

"Can you find your way home?" said Lyn, suddenly understanding the look of watery hopelessness.

"No," said Sharon, in a cross between a wail and a whisper.

Lyn felt a quick surge of excitement – a project – can't possibly go home yet, got to sort this out.

"Where do you live, then?" she said, jogging forgotten, counting forgotten.

Sharon pointed at the massive structure of the Estate. "In number six," she said.

"You have to know more than that," said Lyn. "There's a number six on every level and in every tower. There must be hundreds of number sixes."

Sharon was obviously struggling to keep her mouth from turning down at the corners. Lyn could see that she had suspected as much. So she scraped her short hair back behind her ears, ready for action. "Now," she said, in the most reassuring voice she could manage. "You must have more of an address than six. Are you Johnson, Warner, Barney, Merrick, Parsons or Parker?"

"Parker," said Sharon. "Or Parsons."

"Which though? And Walk or Tower?"

"I'll watch for my dad," said Sharon. "I'll see him get back and I'll go in with him."

"When does he get home?"

"I don't know. It depends. He's a taxi driver."

"You can't rely on your dad to take you home," said Lyn. "What if he doesn't come? I mean, what if he doesn't come till late? You have to be able to find your own way. Now – what do you see out of your windows?"

"Roofs."

"If you look straight down. That main road?"

"No. Two little roads, and a crosssing."

"You're Parsons," said Lyn kindly. "Come on." And she began to skip ahead sideways, past the line of shops and laundrette that ran past the most southerly tower. "I'll take you."

"Won't your mum worry if you don't go straight home?" said Sharon, following her.

"My mum worries whatever I do," said Lyn, "so it doesn't make much odds."

Sharon began to veer towards the nearest tower, and the

entrance that gaped blackly at its foot. "Can't we go in here?" she said.

"No," said Lyn. "We'll go in at Barney. It's better. And keep away from Warner. They'll drop things on you."

Even as she said it, a shower of tiny pebbles smattered down from above. Several of them hit Sharon, and two pinged loudly off the tiny metal attaché case she had brought her sandwiches in. "Ow!" she said, and ran from the base of the tower towards the shops and Lyn.

Lyn was looking up at the small grimacing faces that seemed to sit in a row on a windowsill seven floors above, like so many severed heads. "I don't know where they get the stones from," she said admiringly. "That's the window by Warner Tower lift. They smashed it out weeks ago. That's why we won't go up that way."

"I don't like this," said Sharon.

"The kids are no bother," said Lyn. "But it's best to keep away from some of the older boys."

"How?"

"You'll learn. It's easy."

She was already hoping they'd meet a gang. Or not meet it, exactly, but see it, hear it coming. You could be so quiet when you were so much smaller and younger than they were. Their boots clattered on stone stairs, their hoarse voices echoed up and down the lift shafts. The sounds of their approach always made Lyn feel especially light-weight, especially aware of wearing soft-soled trainers, not boots like theirs, and of being able to whisk around a corner, along a walkway, or up or down a different stair, as fast as she wanted and with no sound at all. Of being able to get out of their way without their ever having known she had been in it.

"It's too early, really," she said. "But I wish some of them'd come along. Then I could show you what to do."

The last shop in the row was the newspaper-cum-sweet shop with a sign outside advertising ice-cream and cold drinks. A clamouring mass of children of various ages clustered around its window and door and spread across their path, right up to the base of the tower that seemed to be called Barne.

"Barne?" said Sharon. "Is that what you mean?"

"Barney," said Lyn. "The Y dropped off last winter." She elbowed her way through the throng, glancing back to make sure Sharon was squeezing through behind her before the bodies closed up together again.

"Where do you live?" said Sharon, as they went in at the doorway at the base of the tower. It was cold inside, and not only because they were cut off from the pale March sunshine. This coldness seemed to be a positive thing that came out of the grey concrete walls in much the same way that light comes out of a neon sign. There was litter on the grey stone stairs, and a sour smell.

Lyn made a face, but not at the smell. The question was an unpleasant reminder of what she was trying to forget. "In a flat in a house down the road," she said, gabbling the words to discourage Sharon from pressing the point. She stopped on the first landing, dimly lit by a window that was too high, too narrow and too dirty to be really effective. "Listen," she said.

"What for?" said Sharon.

"You can hear them going home."

It was true that there were echoing noises, both far and near, that were very likely made by human voices. "Why do we have to stand here and listen?" said Sharon plaintively.

Lyn looked at her, enclosed by stone walls on each side, miserably holding on to one of the chipped metal handrails, and felt a twinge of irritation. Sharon obviously needed to have her mind taken off things, too, so why wouldn't she pay attention to what was going on around her instead of clinging on to her unhappiness in such a soggy way.

"I can hear Tamer shouting," Lyn said. "Come on." She ran up the next flight to where the narrow stone tunnel of the stairway opened out on to a covered walkway. One half of the walkway led directly to the left, the other half diagonally to the right. She took off along the left-hand route, followed by Sharon. There were bright blue doors, evenly spaced, on their right, and a shoulder-high wall on their left. Over the edge of this wall the school, and even half the laundrette, could be seen, two floors below. The walkway led to another tower with a wide stone landing from which a dingy stairway ran both upwards and downwards. There were bright red lift doors, with names and words scrawled all over them in black, set in to the tower wall. Two walkways converged at the same point, so that it was possible to go up, down or sideways from the same starting place. The first walkway ran along the outside of the Estate. The second overlooked an inner court with a playground. Lyn took the second.

"I'll never remember this way home," Sharon wailed at her heels.

"It isn't your way home," said Lyn. "It's Tamer's." They rounded a corner and bumped into a dark boy of about their own age, arguing loudly with two others.

"Tamer!" said Lyn, clouting him on the arm. "Beat you!"

"I wasn't racing you," said Tamer, but he looked peeved. "Which way'd you come?"

"My way," said Lyn.

"Where you going?"

"Come on, Sharon," said Lyn. Then, to Tamer, "We're going to Parsons. Walk probably. But it might be Tower." She turned and led the way back towards the outer walkway and the next flight of stairs up.

"You're going the wrong way, then," Tamer called after them.

"We're not, then," Lyn called back. To Sharon she said, "If Tamer ever tells you you're going the wrong way, you know you're right, OK?"

As they reached the next tower, she caught hold of

Sharon's sleeve and pulled her to the edge of the walkway, just outside the huge archway that opened on to the dim tower landing, with its own lift and stairways. "Now," she said, "is this the right height?"

Sharon peered down at the roads and the crossing below. "No," she said uncertainly.

"Too low?"

"Yes."

"We'll go up by the stairs," said Lyn. "Then we can look over at each level."

At the next level Sharon, leaning over, said hopelessly, "I don't know. It doesn't look right . . ."

"We'll try higher," said Lyn.

But as they chased each other up the next dingy flight a new sound started up, above and behind the traffic noise and the distant calling and running of feet. It was made by voices, but voices which sounded not quite human, nor yet quite animal, either. It seemed to come from the heart of the tower – distant and eerie and desperate. If the entire Estate seemed like a great cold castle, then the voices suggested prisoners long-forgotten in the dungeons below it. At almost the same time, a far far away bell began to ring continuously, like a warning.

Sharon gripped hold of Lyn's wrist and hung on. "It's ghosts!" she said.

Lyn worked her wrist free and laughed – "It isn't ghosts," she said. She ran on up the second half of the flight to the top. "Come on!" she called back, suddenly aware that Sharon's footsteps had not been following. She hung over the railing at the top of the flight and looked down. She could see the small figure, foreshortened by the angle, huddled on the smelly and enclosed little landing formed by the elbow of the stairs. "I can't!" came a whispery voice. "I want to go home."

"I'm *taking* you home," said Lyn. "Come on, will you. It's not ghosts, honestly. I know what it is." She waited but

Sharon seemed unable to move. So she turned away and whisked out of sight, guessing that Sharon would follow rather than be left alone. Sure enough, as she hurried towards the lift doors she could hear a faint padding and sniffing behind her.

As she drew level with the lift doors the wailing grew louder and it became apparent that it wasn't a continuous sound, as it had seemed from below, but a series of cries and calls all blending with each other into a despairing chant. The bell didn't sound much louder from here, but still it rang on.

Lyn banged with her two hands together on the closed lift doors. "What floor are you on?" she yelled at the fine crack where they joined. Sharon walked towards her reluctantly.

"What is it?" she said. And then, with the first spark she'd shown all day, "I wish you'd *explain*."

"Sorry," said Lyn abstractedly. "They're stuck in the lift somewhere, but I don't know where. I'm trying to work it out."

She hit at the solid doors again and screamed at the top of her voice, "WHAT FLOOR?" The lift doors threw her voice straight back at her and sent it riccocheting away past them, and up and down the stairs.

"Oh, is that the alarm bell, then?" said Sharon. "Won't someone come?"

"Not for a long time," said Lyn. "He's a lazy old slob and these things are always getting stuck. He gets bored. You see, you can sometimes open it from the outside if you know what floor. But when I ask all I get is a lot of screaming. Silly idiots."

She rested the side of her head against the doors. "Up, I think," she said, and set off for the next flight. "But you can't really tell. Sound's funny stuff." She heard Sharon stumbling up the stairs behind her. "It's what's so exciting about this place," she said encouragingly. "You never know what you'll meet round a corner."

Sharon, who had given the impression of being on the verge of tears from the first moment she had walked into the school that morning, gave way completely. "I don't *want* to meet anything," she said. "I want to be in my home."

Lyn didn't know what to do with her. If you found someone who was lost and offered to take her home, surely that resolved the problem. And surely she couldn't expect you to abandon a lot of screaming people shut in a lift when you were actually passing them.

"What with them moaning," she said helplessly, "and now you moaning . . ." They'd reached the next level and she went straight to the lift doors. "It could be here," she said. "It doesn't sound much louder, but it could be."

Sharon ran to the edge of the parapet and looked out and then down. "This is it," she said. "I'm here!"

Lyn punched the button in the wall beside the lift, the one with the arrow pointing upwards. Nothing happened. She punched the one below it; the one with the arrow pointing downwards. There was a loud ping, the arrow lit up, and the doors parted by about two inches. Instantly the anguished crying came pouring out of the narrow space. Lyn pressed the down arrow again, and held it. Two seconds later the doors opened fully and five or six Arab women in black veils and face masks surged out. Two of them, still wailing and obviously in tears, supported each other to the stairs and began to ascend. The rest hurried off down the inner walkway towards the flats that faced out on to one of the central courtyards. Their robes shimmered around them so that they looked like figures reflected in water. Within seconds Sharon and Lyn were alone, and the only sound was of the traffic three floors down.

"Well!" said Lyn. "Look at that! They never even said thank you!"

"I know where I am now," said Sharon. She wiped her nose on her sleeve. Her white face had a hint of colour in it. "It's along there. Number six."

"They could have trodden me underfoot for all they cared," said Lyn.

"See you tomorrow," said Sharon. She ran past five blue doors and knocked on the sixth – then looked quickly back at Lyn, tiny in the distance, in terror in case she was wrong. But the door opened and the right face was behind it.

"I expect they were pleased really," Sharon called to Lyn, her voice louder and stronger than it had been all day. Then she went inside.

Lyn gave a quick wave towards the closing blue door. "Something always happens when I come here," she said to herself with satisfaction.

She began to run down the stairs, holding on to the cold scabby handrail and jumping the last three steps in each section. She was perfecting a technique of jumping down the last steps and around the corner to the top of the next flight all in one move. Couldn't be done without the support of the handrail. By the time she reached ground level her right hand was brown with rust.

She'd never opened a jammed lift at Parsons Fourth Level before. It had been easier than Johnson Seventh Level, or Merrick Third. With both of those she'd had to press the button rhythmically several times and then finish off by pressing the other button, the one which pointed in whichever direction the lift had *not* been travelling at the time of its crisis. She herself didn't travel by any of the lifts. It was fun being outside them when they got stuck, boring being inside.

The crowd around the newsagent's door had lessened by now. Only about five stragglers were still waiting outside. Lyn considered dropping in for a Milky Way, then decided against it. She was quite late already and it really was time to go home.

It was only a short walk, it only took four and a half minutes, but with every step a little more of the fun went out of the memory of racing up and down the stone stairs and performing the dramatic rescue of the wailing women. At one point she started to run. Then she stopped and shrugged. "I'm in no hurry," she said to herself. And walked slowly, all the rest of the way.

Chapter Two

Somewhere a sudden spring storm blew up and circled offshore, and then onshore, scattering the white birds into shrieking confusion. As the storm died they reassembled in their raggedy group, feeding and bickering as before, but the one bird had been blown farther out to sea than the rest. In the storm the wind had changed direction, so that it blew strongly offshore, and it pushed the bird farther and farther away, towards the east.

As she drew nearer to the house, Lyn was aware of a movement in its top bay window. Her mother was watching out for her from the sitting room of the flat. She walked more slowly. She didn't look up.

By the time she reached the front door, her mother was already there, holding it open for her. Lyn walked in past her. "'Lo", she said, noticing what her mother was wearing without appearing to look directly at her. She had handed out breakfast that morning in jeans and a baggy sweater, and that was the way she had remained for her morning job in the greengrocer's, but it was afternoon now and so she was wearing a light wool skirt in a misty pattern of lilac and pale blue squares. On top she wore a lilac blouse. Tomorrow she would wear the pale blue blouse with the same skirt. The day after she would most likely go on to the skirt made of misty beige and pale green squares, with the beige blouse or the pale green one. Then the green blouse or the beige one next day, and so back to the lilac and blue. Mix and match. It was what the magazines said you should do,

especially if you didn't have much to spend on clothes. Lyn
found all this reassuring – not so much because her mother
had so obviously got to grips with the right way of organis-
ing her clothes, but because what she was going to wear
next was so predictable. She hadn't always been predictable. Before it had all happened, when she had had
more to spend, you never quite knew what you'd find her
in next. But then, of course, other things had been predictable, so it hadn't mattered.

Her mother followed her up the stairs and in at the open
door of the flat. "It's almost five," she said as she did so.
"Where have you been till this time? I nearly rang the
school, but then I thought no one would answer and that
would only worry me more."

"Someone stuck in the lift," Lyn mumbled. She hurried
in to the sitting room and switched on the television set. She
never told her mother anything about the Estate. Partly
because it was private, partly because she wasn't supposed
to go there unless she was visiting someone. "You got stuck
in a lift?" said her mother, following her. "What lift?" It had
been a mistake to mention a lift, of course. That gave
everything away. "On the Estate?"

Lyn nodded and sat down on the sofa with her feet
drawn up, staring at the screen. If she had sat in her father's
chair she would have had a better view, because his chair
was on one side of the fireplace, pointing directly at the
television which was on the other. When she sat on the
sofa, which stood straight across in front of the fireplace
with its back to the door, she had to twist round a little bit to
see the screen. But she never sat in her father's chair.

Her mother moved over to her and sat down beside her.
"You shouldn't have been playing around on the Estate,"
she said. "You should have come straight home. But I'm
sorry you got stuck – was it frightening?"

"Not me!" said Lyn. "Other people."

"Well, how could other people getting stuck make *you*

late? Lyn? Oh you do make me cross – stop watching that television and answer me."

"I was seeing someone home," said Lyn, without looking round. "I was all right. I don't know what you're on about."

"What I'm on about is that I like to know where you are."

Lyn looked at her for a moment, then smiled. She stood up, turned around, knelt on the sofa and looked over the back of it. Then she pushed her hands down behind the seat cushions she was kneeling on; rocked herself back, tipped the cushions up towards her and peered under them. She looked at her mother again, and shrugged. "I'm sure I'm here somewhere," she said.

Her mother laughed. "Yes, I suppose you are," she said. For a moment she looked relaxed, unanxious, and then – she glanced briefly at the empty chair.

"You always do that," said Lyn.

"Do what?" said her mother, mildly puzzled. She really didn't know.

Lyn turned herself around and flopped down facing the television again. She opened her mouth to say something like, "You keep looking at his chair as if he might be in it . . ." but all that came out was, "What's for tea?"

"I'm making soup. Then there's cheese on toast."

"Not green soup?"

"Watercress soup."

"Yuk!"

"It's not 'Yuk'. It's good for you. It's a spring tonic."

"Why can't we have chips, ever?"

"Because they're bad for you." She got up and went out of the room. After a moment or two Lyn followed her into the large kitchen, leaving the television to talk to itself. It had happened, as always. Her head was full of the thing she didn't want to think about. The chair was empty and was going to stay that way. There was no point in looking at the clock to see if it was nearly time for him to come home because he wasn't coming home; and because of that, the known world was beginning to disintegrate.

"Can I make the cheese on toast?" she said.

"No, and I wish you wouldn't leave that television on when you're not watching it."

"Why can't I make it?"

"Because you don't know how."

The green soup had been passed through the blender and was in an orange-coloured pan on top of the cooker. It looked rather pretty. Lyn found she couldn't say that, either. "Pond water!" she said instead.

Her mother ignored her. She took a block of hard yellow cheese out of the fridge and reached to a shelf above Lyn's head for the cheese grater.

On the work top beside the cooker a tray was laid with cutlery, mats and two glasses of water. Lyn began to take the spoons and knives and forks off the tray, one by one, and to set them on the working top beside it in a pattern. She tried a square, made up of two knives and two forks.

"Mum," she said. "Do we really have to?"

"Have to what?" said her mother. She began to grate cheese at the small kitchen table. The cheese rasped rhythmically against the grater, and the loose table leg knocked against the floor in time with it.

"Have to move?"

"Don't ask silly questions," said her mother. She didn't sound cross. It was simply what she always said when certain matters came up. Rasp, rasp, knock, knock. A long yellow curl of cheese fell to the floor. Lyn picked it up and put it in her mouth. Her mother frowned but didn't say anything.

Lyn began another cutlery square, inside the first one, with the two soup spoons. She opened the cutlery drawer and got out two more spoons to finish off the second part of the pattern. "I really don't want to leave here," she said, patting the spoons gently to align them perfectly.

"Don't you?" said her mother. She tasted the soup and added a small portion of salt. "Lyn, *look* what you've done. I've just laid that tray. Why can't you ever let things be?"

Lyn backed away and watched as the tray was relaid. "Why can't I get the tea sometimes?" she said. "Sue gets theirs about twice a week – decides what to have and everything – "

Her mother took down two bowls from the rack above the cooker where they'd been warming damply in the steam from the heating soup. She had her lilac back to Lyn as she set the bowls on the tray and then dipped a mug into the orange pan and poured green liquid into them. "When you grow up and have to get meals every day you won't think it's such fun," she said.

"I don't mean I want to play at it," said Lyn. "I mean I want to do it properly."

Her mother picked up the tray and carried it through to the sitting room, where she set it on the small dining table. When Lyn's father had been at home, the two leaves had been pulled out at the table, so that it became twice its size. She set out mats, bowls, spoons and water glasses. "If you wanted to help," she said mildly, "you wouldn't have unlaid the tray I'd just laid. Let's have it while it's hot."

She leaned the now empty tray against the wall beside her chair. It had a picture, under its shiny surface, of a huge bunch of flaming poppies and greenery in an orange jug. It clashed rather with the lilac and pale blue.

"I don't want any."

"Don't be silly."

Her mother sat down and Lyn sat down, automatically, opposite her. The poppies with their fierce black centres frowned out from the leaning tray. "I want to stay here, Mum," said Lyn. "I know it here. Why can't we stay?"

Her mother was stirring her soup slowly, watching the

swirl of darker green made by the passage of the spoon. "How do you suppose we can afford to do that?" she said gently.

A wonderful opportunity seemed to Lyn to present itself for consideration. "Can't we go and live on the Estate?" she said. "Isn't that cheaper?"

"You know it's all settled," said her mother. "Please be good about it. You're old enough to know this isn't an easy time for me, and you can help by being co-operative and not arguing all the time. You know we must go and live near Gran and Grandpop so that I can work full-time and you can go to them for your tea – and in the holidays."

"But that's up north," said Lyn. She could feel tears coming up at the backs of her eyes and in her throat, hot spiky tears, like swellings that would go on growing uncomfortably until they burst. Oddly, they seemed to have more to do with anger than with sorrow.

"You'll soon make new friends up there."

"I don't even know what the flat's like," said Lyn.

"I don't know how you can say that. I've described it to you in minute detail. It's nice. You'll like it."

"This is nice. I like this."

"It isn't all that different, really, except that it has a shop under it instead of another flat. It's like a cross between this one and Gran and Grandpop's one. I just wish we didn't have to go through this conversation every other evening. Look, let's finish the soup. Missing a meal isn't going to do any good, one way or another."

Lyn didn't want to eat soup but she didn't want to cry, either. She knew that she would cry if she didn't do something to take her mind off it, and she couldn't think of anything else to do. So she ate the soup. As it went down her throat it felt as though it had corners. It occurred to her that her mother might be having as much difficulty as she was, but she didn't look across at her for fear of seeing that she was right.

When the bowls were empty her mother said, "Please don't be so unhappy about it, Lyn."

"Why couldn't I have come up with you – chosen the flat with you?"

"I didn't want you to miss school."

"At a weekend."

"It was too expensive, two fares."

"I could have gone free with you, on the train."

"Not on the coach, though, and the coach was cheaper."

"When Sue and her mum moved, Sue went with her to see the new places, she was there when they chose, she helped decide."

"Yes, well I think your friends are too much involved in things sometimes. It's all very well, all this doing things, but it's taking away childhood. This is supposed to be a time when you don't have any worries. It's my problem, not yours."

"It'll be my home, too."

"Well, of course it will. That's why I've chosen somewhere you'll like. I've told you – your bedroom looks out at the back, across the allotments and the railway line." She winked at Lyn. "See how well I know you? Not everyone would think that was an advantage, but I know you will. And in case there isn't time to decorate it all before we move in, Grandma's going to do your room first."

Her hopes raised by the wink, Lyn said, "Let me choose the colours? Please?"

"Grandma's got the paper and paint all ready. It's her surprise for you." She got up and walked briskly out of the room. "Cheese on toast in three minutes," she said.

"I don't want any," said Lyn. "I'm going to do my painting."

Three days ago she had begun a picture of the Estate – or at least the view of it she had from her bedroom window. She was painting it more carefully than anything she had ever done before. So far she had completed four out of the six towers and she felt she could finish it tonight. She went into her bedroom to fetch the little glass water pot. As she took it in to the bathroom to fill it, her mother called through from the kitchen, "Have this first."

"No thanks," Lyn called back. She had only lately discovered that the colours of things change according to the time of day and the quality of the light. "I want to do this while the light is right."

"While the *light* is right," came her mother's voice, scornful, and laughing to soften the scorn. But she didn't push the point.

Lyn sat on her bed and looked across the roofs of the two-storey houses opposite, to where the Estate rose up almost as though it would like to eat them. She hadn't included these houses. In fact they interested her so little that she didn't quite understand why, in the picture, the Estate seemed to have no ground level. She was hardly aware that the houses were hiding it. She had an idea, which she knew didn't make any sense at all, that if she concentrated really hard on her painting, she would hear a key in the front door and her father would walk in. He often had come home at this sort of time – though not every day. Sometimes he hadn't come home for several days, once he'd been away nearly two weeks. He worked for a cement company and he often had to go to different building sites, all over the country, to explain why the cement his company made was better for their purposes than any other. Once or twice he'd had to go and look at problems – places where the cement seemed to be failing in some way, and try to work out what was wrong. Those were the occasions when he was away for longer.

"Why don't you tell them to make the cement properly in the first place," Lyn had said once. "Then you won't have to go and sort out all these problems."

He had pretended to be shocked. "The cement is always perfect," he had said. "That's the first thing you learn when you go to work for the company. It only fails if it's used badly, or in the wrong place."

The fact that he had been away from home on business so often made it easy to pretend that he might, after all, come home again. There had been gaps before – this might be another of them – much longer than usual, it was true, but still perhaps only a gap.

The door would open and he would come in and quite soon they'd all be laughing. There'd always been a lot of laughing when he was around. "You mustn't take life seriously," he used to say. "You'll never get out of it alive anyway." If her mother was in one of her anxious moods she sometimes took a while to join in the laughing, but he always won her over in the end. Often by doing something quite stupid.

Once, when Lyn had been perfectly well aware that her parents had been having a row about something, speaking quietly but angrily in the kitchen with the door shut, her father had suddenly walked out of the kitchen, paused for a moment in the tiny hallway, then walked into the sitting room where Lyn was watching television, settled himself in his chair and picked up the paper without a word. When her mother had joined them in front of the TV a few moments later, he had still not said a word and Lyn had felt a sick sinking feeling in her stomach. This must be a row that was going to go on for a while she had thought, this must be serious.

Then she and her mother had noticed it at the same time. Her father, reading the paper solemnly, had discarded his shoes somewhere and was wearing brown leather gloves on his feet. He looked like some kind of weird bird, or perhaps a rather thin frog. Lyn had begun to giggle at once – her mother had frowned briefly and then surprised herself with a sudden snort of laughter. In a slow and stately movement he had crossed one thin leg over the other so that one curiously fingered foot hung in the air, beating time gently. "No one takes me seriously," had come a plaintive voice from behind the paper. They'd laughed on and off for most of the evening after that. The memory kept coming back long after the gloves had been replaced in the drawer in the hallstand.

Lyn, wanting all that back again, worked at her painting as though it was a magic rite – as though, if she was attentive and made a good job of the picture, she would find she had conjured him up, as people were supposed to conjure up ghosts. Although she didn't honestly believe it would work – although she was old enough to know that being good and doing well doesn't always get you what you want – she couldn't help trying, just in case.

But she had left it a little too late. The sky, which yesterday had been light grey, was tonight a deep charcoal colour. The lights, which yesterday had shone in just a few windows, tonight shone in most. She looked at her painted tower outlines, the result of so much care and careful mixing of colour, and saw unimpressive smears. The addition of a tiny bit of green to the grey which yesterday had seemed such a triumph, today looked muddy and silly, and the thick blobs of undiluted white, which yesterday had seemed so exactly to suggest the brightness of those light bulbs which actually remained intact on the lift landings, today looked like nothing but thick blobs of undiluted white.

"Stupid, useless picture," said Lyn, and tore the sheet of paper loudly off its pad, then in half.

"What's the matter? Is the light wrong?" said her mother in the doorway, amused.

Lyn put the two halves of paper together and tore them in half again. Then she put those pieces together and tore them once more, and again, and again, each tear harder work, each result smaller and thicker.

Seeing that she was crying, her mother sat on the bed beside her and stroked her hair. "You'll like it up north," she said. "You'll like seeing more of Gran and Grandpop."

Lyn ducked her head out from under the stroking hand.

"When am I going to see my dad again?" she said. She hadn't really wanted to ask in case she didn't like the answer, but she couldn't help herself. Because he wasn't a ghost, who might be drawn back by magic, he was alive; it was just that he chose to live somewhere else now. The divorce was all over; not that it, in itself, had seemed to Lyn to be much of an event. It had turned out to be something that happened secretly, arranged by strangers who could do what was necessary without getting upset.

"As soon as the move is over," said her mother. "As soon as we're all settled down in our new lives."

"Him, too?"

"Him, too. All of us. Then we'll get it organised. There'll be arrangements." She touched Lyn's cheek lightly. "He's still your father. He still loves you."

That night Lyn had a nightmare. At least, she thought it must have been a nightmare. She couldn't remember anything about it. All she knew was that she woke herself up screaming, "Tell me, tell me." And when her mother came in to comfort and reassure her, she went on saying, "Tell me, tell me," for several minutes – although she could no longer remember what it was that she so much wanted to be told.

Chapter Three

"I know something you don't know," said Mandy Wilson to Lyn.

"I doubt it," said Lyn

"Your dad's left your mum," said Mandy with relish, "And you've got to get out of your flat. My mum's coming round to help you pack."

"Of course I know about it," said Lyn with the utmost scorn. They were in the big school recreation room which had chairs all down one side and shiny parallel bars on the wall opposite. It was after lunch, and Minna had been handing round slices of her birthday cake. "Just because I know something doesn't mean I have to talk to you about it, if I don't want to."

"If you know so much," said Mandy, "when do you move, then?"

"Mind your own business, why can't you?" said Lyn.

Mandy's eye was drawn back to the three uneaten portions of chocolate fudge-filled sponge. "Your mum makes good cakes," she said to Minna.

"I made it myself," said Minna. "And you're not getting any more. There's other people who haven't had any yet."

One of the people who hadn't had any yet was Sharon. She hadn't even eaten her own lunch, packed by her mother into the tin attaché case that morning. She had told Minna it was because she was homesick. "This is your home now," Minna had said, in motherly tones. Sharon's white, lost face had folded itself into a scowl. "It doesn't feel like it," she'd muttered. Lyn, overhearing, had felt first scornful and then uneasy. She wondered if moving house always made you pale and feeble like Sharon. Then she became aware that Sue was standing quite close to her, licking thick chocolatey stickiness off her fingers. When she'd done licking she said, "You didn't tell me." She sounded reproachful.

Lyn grasped a handful of Sue's green cardigan and pulled her away from Mandy and everyone else, towards the door and the hooks where all the coats hung. "Let's not talk about it in front of poxy Mandy Wilson," she said, when they were well out of earshot.

"OK," said Sue. "But I'd have thought you'd have told me. I told you when it was my parents."

"I'm sorry," said Lyn. "I didn't think *anyone* knew. I'd have told you first – honestly."

"How long has it all been going on?" said Sue. She still looked hurt.

"Ages. I just wasn't ready to think about it yet."

Sue nodded sympathetically. "You never will be ready to think about it," she said. "I remember. Did you know it might happen? Is that why your dad was away so much?"

"It might be. I thought it was for his work."

Sue shrugged. "You can't tell, can you?" she said. "Has he got – you know – someone else?"

"That's what she said. I don't get given details. I don't really know."

"Let's go to the bridge," said Sue.

"Is there time?"

"Bound to be. We can run."

They slipped out of the recreation room, sidled through the leaping, chasing figures in the playground, and then fled down the road, round a corner, and up the steep pavement which curved over the railway bridge. Once there, they hitched themselves on to the parapet by their elbows, where they hung, like dolls. The toes of their shoes scraped and tapped against the brickwork and their heads craned forwards to look over and down at the shining tracks. The tracks ran towards their bridge and out of sight beneath it, ready to carry the tube trains underground after their journey through the daylight which shone on the outer reaches of the system.

From here they could see the signals, half the station, and about a hundred metres of double track. The station was covered with a canopy, made of glass, which was supposed to let the light reach the two platforms; but this glass was so encrusted with dirt and pigeon droppings that very little got through and the platform lights were only turned off on the brightest of days. Because the glass was so filthy, the only passengers they could watch properly were the ones who stood at the extreme ends of the platforms, nearest to them. However, it was often possible to see the lower halves of the people who stood just a little further in, and to speculate on what their top halves might be like.

"He'll have green hair, I bet he will, look at those trousers," said Lyn.

"Rubbish!" said Sue. "They're quite ordinary. I bet it's just a mucky brown colour, like ours."

"We'll never know, anyway," said Lyn. "He's waiting for a train going the other way."

"We wouldn't know even if he was coming this way. Unless you reckon you've got X-ray eyes and can see through the roof."

"You can often see their heads."

"Their heads!" said Sue. "When they're inside? Course you can't!"

"You can if they lean them on the window to go to sleep," said Lyn.

"Oh, that's only the ones who are on the train already. Even if he was coming this way, he's not going to get in, lean his head on the window, and go off to sleep, bam, just like that, is he?"

"He might if he's tired," said Lyn.

"No one could be that tired. Not at lunchtime."

"Could be, if he'd had lunch in a pub. A dozen pints and he'd be right off."

"Nar! He's not a beer drinker. He's too thin. My uncle says beer drinkers are fat."

"You can only see his thin legs," said Lyn. "He might have a great big beer belly, just out of sight."

"Not on those little whippety legs. They'd snap in half."

They had to drop down from the wall for a moment or two, because it was too tiring, laughing and hanging on at the same time.

While they were giggling on the pavement, a train came rattling up from the distance and stopped in the station. They hitched themselves rapidly back to their vantage point as the doors sighed open. But nobody much seemed to get in or out, or nobody they could see, anyway. The thin legs on the opposite platform had paced impatiently out of sight for the moment. The train doors sighed shut again, and after a pause, the whole thing started up and clattered towards them, vibrating loudly as it passed under the bridge and went on its way.

"It's a bit dull at lunchtime," said Sue. "Evening rush hour's better. Do you want to swap cardigans?"

"*Can* we?"

"Just for this afternoon."

Sue's green cardigan was everything a cardigan should be; made of synthetic fibre and shop-bought. Lyn's was pure wool, hand-knitted by her mother. So it wasn't a fair swap and Lyn was very grateful for the offer.

When, Lyn now in green and Sue in knitted navy, they were hanging back on the wall again, Sue said, "Are you really moving?"

Lyn didn't answer at once. The divorce was bad enough – it was the move that was unthinkable. However, now that Mandy had publicised it she could hardly hope to ignore it any longer. Anyway, she wanted to reassure Sue that she really did deserve the generous gesture.

"Yes," she said. "Up north, near my gran and grandpop."

"But what for?"

"We can't afford the flat without my dad, she says. Rents are lower up there and she can work full-time if I go to them after school."

"My mum works full-time down here. I've got a key."

"Yes, well. That's you, isn't it. She won't leave me alone, will she? I tell you – when I'm grown-up and married with kids she'll still want to see me across the road."

"She lets you cross the *road* on your own!"

"I suppose so. But only just."

A distant roaring and vibrating soon resolved itself into another train, travelling the same way as the previous one. It stopped at the platform for the usual length of time, although there was no blur of movement from beneath the grimy glass roof.

"Routine stopping time," said Sue. "Must keep on schedule."

"Mustn't be early, mustn't be late," said Lyn.

"Or else BAM, SMASH, CRUNCH, SPLINTER," they both shouted together.

The thin legs on the other platform paced briefly into their sight and out of it again.

"Getting bored," said Lyn. "If his hair isn't green already, he'll probably decide to dye it now, just to cheer himself up."

"I'll tell you something I've just thought of," said Sue seriously.

"I'll tell *you* something," said Lyn. "That's two trains one way and nothing through from under us. You know what that means?"

"Something's stuck," said Sue gleefully.

"Signal failure," said Lyn

"Those signals are working. Points failure?"

"Or power failure?"

"No, can't be power failure," said Sue. "They'd stop both ways. Wouldn't they?"

"Body on the line," said Lyn, dropping down from the wall.

"Do you think so?"

"Might be."

"Come on," said Sue, and dashed across the road to lean on the opposite parapet. From here they could see roughly another hundred or so metres of track which sloped downwards away from them, the embankment walls rising more steeply each side, until the tracks disappeared into the black hole that was the mouth of the tunnel. "No body between here and the tunnel," said Sue.

"You don't really wish there was, do you?"

"No," said Sue. "Anyway, it can't be that, because they'd switch off all the power, both ways."

"I think I can see the train, down the tunnel," said Lyn. "If you stare and stare and narrow your eyes can you see a sort of glow?"

"I think so."

"That's the light from the driver's cab. I'm sure it is. They're only just inside the tunnel and I bet they think they're miles underground. I just hope they're not like the lot in the lift yesterday."

"What lot?"

"Oh, a lot of women. The lift got stuck and I let them out, but all they could do was scream and wail. It must be deafening in there if there's women like that on that train."

"It probably hasn't stopped for long," said Sue. "They wouldn't be yelling yet."

"Don't you believe it," said Lyn. "That lot would yell at once."

"Hey!" called Sue, at the distant tunnel mouth. "You're all walled in! Buried alive! You'll all be turned into ghouls and you'll walk the night forever, moaning in the tunnels."

Lyn turned her back on the view and leaned on the parapet. "I'll miss you," she said.

"I remember what I thought of just now," said Sue, turning to lean beside her. "Your mum mustn't move out of the flat until everything's settled. I remember my mum being told that. If she goes before it's fixed up, I think your dad can take the flat or something, and leave you with nothing at all."

Lyn's mouth dragged down at the corners, despite her efforts to stop it. "It is fixed up," she said. "It's done. They are divorced. Anyway, my dad wouldn't do that."

"No, course he wouldn't," said Sue. "Look! Here comes the train!" A gust of air rushed out of the tunnel and pushed two pigeons off the line in a confusion of flapping. Immediately behind it came the train, not very fast, ready to pass under their bridge and stop at the platform for the thin-legged traveller. "Just a little scare, folks," Sue called at its roof as it disappeared underneath them. "Not the real thing this time – that'll be another day."

"We ought to get back," said Lyn.

They jogged back the way they'd come, elbows tight to their sides, fists clenched, pushing their breath out in exaggerated little puffs.

"When do you move?" said Sue, giving up on the fake puffing. "Hey, I don't want you to go."

"I don't know exactly. Soon. She's vague about the date. Something to do with people moving out of the flat we're moving in to." She kicked out briefly at the base of a lamp-post as she passed it. "She never really properly tells me *anything*," she said.

"Perhaps she takes after you!" Sue said.

"Oh belt up," said Lyn guiltily.

"I'd like to be in charge of the underground system one day," said Sue wistfully, as they turned in at the playground under the shadow of the Estate towers. "First thing I'd do would be order a whole load of new rolling stock that wouldn't pack up in tunnels."

Chapter Four

The bird was pushed by unusually steady winds for hundreds, and then thousands, of miles. It survived. It was a powerful flier, and in any case could rest and feed on the sea.

When it first saw land again, it wasn't unduly impressed by it. It flew straight over it until, on the other side, it encountered a sandy shore that was more to its liking. Not that it bothered with the sand. It kept well out to sea, where the fishing was as good as any it had found before.

For the next week or so, nothing much more seemed to happen. School went on as usual. Mandy Wilson, finding that Lyn didn't bother to react to her comments on divorce and absent fathers, lost interest. Sue was sympathetic enough not to bring the subject up.

Her father's chair remained empty and humourless. Neither Lyn nor her mother ever sat in it. Lyn did her best not even to look at it, and was usually successful – it was only when her mother had long telephone conversations with her grandparents, in the bedroom with the door shut, that her eyes began to turn towards it. She tried to concentrate on whatever was on television, but couldn't because she kept wondering what they were talking about. Not that she didn't know, of course, it was just that she didn't know exactly.

One evening when the bedroom door clicked open again, her mother didn't reappear in the sitting room, as she usually did, but called from where she was. Before Lyn had had time to uncurl her legs and stand up, she called again, "Lyn hurry, this is long distance." As Lyn scooted on one foot around the frame of the bedroom door she saw her mother standing up by the bed, in front of a crushed circle on the creamy bedcover where she had been sitting, holding the receiver out towards her at the full stretch of the cord – as though vital seconds would be saved by this tiny lessening of the distance between it and her daughter.

"Gran says she hasn't spoken to you for ages," she said as Lyn took the receiver, "and don't sit on the bed."

"I'm only sitting on your creases," said Lyn.

"What, lovey?" came her grandmother's voice through the earpiece.

"Hallo, Gran," said Lyn.

Her mother went out of the room – but didn't shut the door.

"How are you, lovey?" said the telephone voice. Lyn didn't know if it was her imagination or if her grandmother really was talking to her in an unusually sympathetic tone, rather as you might talk to somebody who had been ill.

"OK," said Lyn.

"I hope you're as excited as we are about you coming to live up here?"

"Yes," said Lyn. No point in saying anything else. "When do we come, exactly?"

"Soon, lovey, very soon. And you'll be starting a whole new life up here. That'll be exciting, won't it?"

"Yes," said Lyn flatly. The response seemed to be all part of the question – she didn't feel any need to try and think up something different.

"I'm all ready to start decorating your new bedroom, just as soon as the flat's free. So it'll be freshly done when you come up. That'll be . . . "

". . . . exciting," said Lyn.

There was a laugh. "Sorry, lovey, do I keep saying that? You're not very easy to talk to on the phone – you just say yes."

"No!" said Lyn.

Another laugh. "I think you'll like the school here, it's got a much larger playing field than yours, your mother says."

"Oh," said Lyn, and now she did search around in her mind for something to say. Her grandmother was right, it wasn't fair to let her do all the work. "And when we're settled my dad'll come and see us," she said.

There was a brief pause. "Well, we won't worry about that just now," said her grandmother. "I'll have to go, Lyn, Grandpop's waving his wallet at me, he thinks I'm extravagant on the phone – what? – oh yes – Grandpop's blowing you a kiss, Lyn."

"Thanks," said Lyn.

"And one from me. Goodbye, lovey, see you soon, love to Mummy."

"Goodbye," said Lyn.

She didn't put the receiver down at once because she knew it would make the bell in the tiny hall ping and her mother would know the call was over and start talking. She didn't want to talk until she had worked out why she suddenly felt so odd. She felt as though something was falling away from her, like a stone dropped down a deep well, bouncing off the sides as it falls, the sound growing softer as the distance increases until it plops in to the water at the bottom and is gone.

The telephone burred a loud complaint at being parted from its rest and she replaced it. The feeling had been set off by what her grandmother had said, or perhaps by what she had not said. The stone that was falling away, falling irretrievably into the distant water, was her father.

Lyn went back into the sitting room. Her mother was sitting in the corner of the sofa with her feet tucked up under her, looking at the newspaper. She smiled briefly but didn't really look up.

Lyn sat down on the floor, more or less beside her, leaning her back against the sofa. "I don't think Gran expects Dad to come and see us up there," she said.

"If you want to talk to me," said her mother, folding the paper back on itself to make it easier to hold, "turn the television off first. I can't hear you."

Lyn crawled across the floor to the set, turned the sound down by the smallest amount she could manage, and repeated what she had said.

"You can't expect your grandmother to want to talk about your father. Not now."

"I don't see why not."

"Oh, Lyn, really!"

"When is he coming, then?"

"When we're settled."

"When is he coming here?" said Lyn loudly and, she knew, unreasonably.

"He isn't coming back here."

"He's probably just away on business," said Lyn, "that's all. When does he get back from on-business?"

"You go on like this," said her mother, "and then you wonder why I don't always rush to tell you things. He lives somewhere else now."

Lyn, who was still kneeling on the floor, leant forward and turned the volume up full on the television set. A truly amazing noise filled the room. "I want to see him," she screamed above it. "I want him to tell me where he lives and why he doesn't want us."

Her mother jumped to her feet, letting the paper fall on to the floor, then strode across the room, the hem of the beige and green skirt flicking painfully across Lyn's ear as she passed. She bent to switch the television off, and then crouched on the floor beside her daughter. "Now listen once and for all," she said, firmly but not it seemed crossly. "Your father lives somewhere else now. He's found someone he loves better than me, but he still loves you, and as soon as we're settled, in the new flat, he'll drive up every other weekend and see you, take you out. But we must wait until we're moved. Otherwise there's just too much upheaval going on all at once. All right? Is that clear now?"

Lyn, kneeling on the floor, avoiding looking at her mother crouching by her side, felt as though she had somehow slid backwards through her life and become, by mistake, three or four years younger than she really was.

"Can I go and stay with him? After we've moved?" she said, as calmly as she could.

"Yes, you can." Her mother stood up. "I'm going to get the tea," she said. In the sitting room doorway she paused. "You can go and stay with him and his new – wife," she said. "And see their little baby." Even as she spoke she disappeared out of the doorway – standing there all misty browns and greens one minute, gone the next.

Lyn stood up quickly to find that her right foot was numb. She stood for a moment shaking it, waiting for it to rejoin her, which it did with horrible crawling sensations, almost as though small water creatures were burrowing up through her veins. "I don't want to see any baby," she shouted while she waited, but there was no response.

She limped into the kitchen and stood in the doorway. "I don't want to see any baby," she said again.

"Well, you'll have to, if you want to visit your father," said her mother briskly, breaking eggs neatly into a bowl, her back to Lyn. "They all live together." She opened the drawer in the kitchen table, pulling it out far and hard so that the loose leg hobbled in protest. She began to rake around amongst the pieces of cutlery inside. "He's your half-brother," she said, selecting a whisk and pushing the drawer shut in three awkward stages. It always stuck if it was rushed.

Lyn had heard the term half-brother before but had never really thought out what it meant. Now it sounded peculiar – like something not quite human. If half of it was her brother, then what was the other half? "Why have they got it?" she said, appalled. "Whatever for?"

"It's hardly unusual for people who get married to have a baby," said her mother, beating the eggs with a hand whisk so that her voice was hard to hear. "You know that well enough."

"Did you know they were going to?"

"It isn't my business what they do. Pass me the toma-toes from beside you, will you Lyn. They're in that brown paper bag."

Lyn passed them. "How old is it?" she said, won-dering vaguely how it was possible to feel surprised and blank at the same time.

"Only a few weeks," said her mother, chopping the tomatoes on the small chopping board, the one with the flowers carved all over the handle, the one they'd all bought together from a National Trust shop when they'd visited that big house and garden. "But he'll grow." Her voice began to sound different – not strained now but bright and encouraging. "You're his big sister," she said. "It'll be nice for him to have you to play with him."

Lyn scuffed her feet on the kitchen doorstep – at the point where the green hall carpet met the brown lino tiles. She pushed at the door frame which had begun to annoy her just by being there. "I could play rolling it down the stairs," she said.

"Just stop that," said her mother, dropping chopped tomato into the beaten egg. "You're being silly."

Lyn knew perfectly well she was being silly, but somehow she couldn't stop it. "I could take it to the swimming baths and play see-if-it-floats," she said. "I could take it up to the roof and play see-if-it-flies."

She found that she so disliked the person she was at that moment, standing all hunched and crooked in the doorway saying such awful things, that she began to cry. Not so much at the thought of her father wearing gloves on his feet to make the new baby laugh, as because she didn't want to be in the same body as the person who seemed to have charge of it at the moment.

Her mother simply continued to make the omelette, and refused to discuss the baby any further.

Chapter Five

For three or four days after the revelation about the baby, time seemed to slip back into its nothing-much-happening phase. It was almost as if the whole thing had been a peculiar game, as though nothing that had been said had really meant anything at all. Because of this the next stage, when it came, seemed sudden and shocking.

A few days before school ended for the Easter holidays, Lyn's mother told her that she should spend her evening sorting out and packing her belongings. "I'll see to your clothes," she said. "I want you to do your books and toys and paints and things. I've put some cardboard boxes in your room."

"You should have asked me," said Lyn, following her to the door of the bedroom and looking in at the assorted cartons. "I could have got these. They have lots outside the Off-Licence on the Estate."

"These came from the shop. Oh it's all right," as Lyn tipped up the nearest one and looked suspiciously into its corners, "I've shaken out all the dirt."

"OK, I'll do it," said Lyn. "We're about off, are we?"

"About, yes. Day after tomorrow. You're going to miss the end of term, but you won't mind that too much, will you?"

"*Going* the day after tomorrow? You mean tomorrow's my last day at school?"

"No – I don't pick up the hired car until four on Friday. You can go in tomorrow and the next day."

Lyn pushed the boxes aside with her foot to clear a path to her bed so that she could sit on the edge of it. "You could have told me," she said. "I have got people to say goodbye to, you know."

"I am telling you," said her mother reasonably. "It isn't going to take you more than two days to say goodbye, is it? You don't want to prolong these things and get morbid about them."

Lyn shrugged, and then frowned. "Why are we doing my things first?" she said. "I haven't got much. There's all the other stuff – heaps of it – shouldn't we start on that first?"

"Don't worry about that. Mrs Wilson and her sister are coming in tomorrow to help me with all that."

Lyn remembered what Mandy Wilson had said all those days ago. "My mum's coming round to help you pack." She felt angry with herself for not having said something straightaway – it was probably too late now. But worth a try. "I can help you," she said. "We can do it together."

"You must go to school – you want to say goodbye."

"I'll go in one lunchtime and say it. Mum, we *can* do it together. I don't want that Mrs Wilson touching our things." Mandy Wilson's mother *and* her aunt – picking things over – telling Mandy what they'd found – Mandy stomping round at school announcing importantly, "My mother says they've got cheap china and half of it cracked. My mother says none of their towels match." The image was intolerable.

Her mother moved over to sit beside her on the bed. She was wearing her harassed expression and she sighed as she sat down. "Nothing is ever straightforward with you, is it?" she said. "It's been agreed for a long time and it's extremely kind of them to help. There's a lot, as you say, even in this small flat there's a lot. It'll take the three of us all day and perhaps part of the next. Everything's got to be wrapped up and put in the tea-chests in the right order – it isn't a question of just gathering it up and flinging it in the way you tidy stuff into your cupboards."

"Well, I know that. That's only clothes. I wouldn't do that with breakables. Why can't Mrs West help you?" Sue's mother would come as a friend not as a trespasser.

"There's not room for anyone else – and they offered first."

"I bet they did."

"Just let it be, can you? I'm letting you pack your own things, I thought you'd be pleased about that, but these days you never seem pleased with anything I do. You're very hard on me, Lyn."

"OK, OK," said Lyn, who hadn't really expected to be able to deflect Mrs Wilson at this late stage. "I'll do it, don't worry. Why's that box got a big red cross on it?"

"Oh yes, I was going to tell you about that. Put the things you want often in that. The rest will be going in to store for a little while."

"Why?"

"Because we can't move in to the new place at once."

"Why not?"

"We can't move in until the other people have moved out. They've got problems with their new house and it's holding things up. It won't be for long."

"Can't we just stay here with everything? Till we can move in?"

"I don't think the new tenants will be very pleased to find us here when they arrive, do you?"

"Well, where will we go?"

"We've been lent a little house."

"What – near Gran and Grandpop?"

"A lot nearer than we are now – about forty miles from them, I think. It's on the coast – by the sea."

"Where?"

"Oh," said her mother vaguely, "the North-East coast. I'll show you on a map sometime."

"Does my dad know? Does he know that address, there?"

"He'll have our address as soon as we're properly settled. Don't look so horrified, it'll be like a holiday."

"Is there anything else I ought to know?" said Lyn. "You

keep throwing things at me – it gets worse and worse – what else is there?"

"Don't shout, there's no need for the whole street to hear."

"I never know what's going on."

"I don't know how you can say that. I was so careful to explain everything. I *told* you why your father was going, I *told* you about the divorce, I *told* you why we had to move, I've described every window and shelf in that flat. Weren't you listening to me, or what?"

"You didn't tell me about the baby."

Her mother got up quickly and went to the doorway. "What was there to say?" she said without looking back. "You know where babies come from."

She turned out of the bedroom in the direction of the sitting room.

Lyn stood up and sidled through the corridor she had made between the waiting boxes. "You didn't tell me about going somewhere else before we move properly," she called from her doorway.

"It's only for a short time, it hardly counts," came the voice from the sitting room. "And if you want to talk to me, come in here, don't shout all over the flat."

Once, when they had been shouting to each other from room to room like this, her father had said mildly, "Give me two cans and a bit of string and I'll set up an intercom system for you." He had said it as though it was a joke – not as though he was really irritated – but perhaps he had been. Perhaps I am awkward, Lyn thought. Perhaps we both are. Perhaps that's why he left. But that was not a thought she wanted to pursue, so she turned her attention to the cardboard boxes.

The move was true after all, it seemed, not a game, not something that could be forgotten. The baby, then, must also be true. There were photographs in the family album which her grandmother kept – photographs which were often brought out at Christmas time. Some were of events which she could remember – Christmases or summer holidays when she had been smaller and younger but still recognisable. She liked looking at those – she liked to be reminded how she had grown, liked to pretend she was an older and wiser sister looking back at her little-sister self. Some had been taken even longer ago and showed a fat toothless baby which she could scarcely believe was her. A baby in her father's arms, a baby balanced on her father's shoulders with one fat leg stretched out on each side of his face under his ears, a baby sitting on a rug on the beach looking with round surprised eyes at her father who was making a funny face at her. She knew it was her, because she had been told so, but somehow she didn't completely believe it. It could be any baby. It could be this new half-brother.

She thought back to the photographs and hoped she wouldn't have to see them again too soon. He was her father, how could he possibly be someone else's father, too? She was sorry she had asked to go and stay with him. If he wanted to see her, he must be by himself.

Her bedroom looked odd when she had finished. She didn't like it, so she spent the ten or so minutes before going to bed staring out of the windows at the Estate. She noted the lighted windows, who was in and who was out. Sometimes she watched a lift rise and tried to guess who might be coming home from work so late – Sharon's father, done with taxi-ing; Tamer's father, through with selling burglar alarms; Leila's mother, back from the telephone exchange.

But the next day when she got home from school it was not only her bedroom which looked odd, but the whole flat. More than odd, it looked extraordinary. Frightening.

As she walked up the road towards the house, she saw them, Mandy's mother and her aunt standing on the tiny path up to the front door – her own mother in the doorway. As she came within earshot she could hear her mother's voice thanking the other two – over and over – while they said it had been no trouble, and what were friends for. It was as though they were all performing some kind of ritual and none of them knew when to stop.

Lyn's arrival on the pathway broke the spell, and they all stopped bobbing and smiling at each other, and bobbed and smiled at her instead.

"They've been very kind," said her mother, as she watched them begin their walk down the road, before following Lyn up the stairs to the flat.

They might have been kind – they had certainly been busy. The flat looked like a nightmare of itself. For some curious reason, Lyn was struck first of all by the rectangles of lighter coloured wall paper where once had been pictures. For a moment it seemed to her that the pictures had been atomised by a ray gun, each leaving behind not a shadow but its exact opposite. Then she saw that there were no curtains at the windows, no ornaments or books on the shelves, and that the centre of the sitting room floor was taken up by six large wooden tea-chests, filled with newspaper-wrapped parcels. There were tea-chests in her mother's room, too, and the kitchen looked the starkest of all. The spice rack was gone, and so was the row of slotted spoons and fish slices which had hung on the wall, and the jars of wooden spoons, and the knife rack, and the cookery books – and all the doors stood open showing empty cupboards.

"It looks terrible," said Lyn. She started to cry before she realised she was going to. "I hate it. Everything's packed, and I haven't even said goodbye to things."

Her mother put her arm around her. "You don't have to say goodbye to things, they're coming with us," she said. "It's all done now. All you have to decide is whether we have fish and chips tonight and hamburgers tomorrow, or hamburgers tonight and fish and chips tomorrow."

She watched Lyn as she spoke. Take-away food with

chips was a rare treat, not usually allowed, let alone encouraged. But all Lyn could say was, "Can we eat it there? Not bring it away?"

"If we eat it there our hair and clothes will smell of grease," said her mother, her smile fading. "You know what it's like."

"Not at the hamburger place. That doesn't smell. Let's go there, it's horrible here."

Her mother considered. "All right," she said eventually. "I suppose it is. But I'll have to go and get tidied up first."

"I want to make a cake," said Lyn suddenly.

"Don't be silly, you don't know how."

"I want to make a cake, to take in tomorrow, when I say goodbye."

"Everything's packed away and I can't start getting stuff out again now. Please be reasonable, Lyn. I know it's all very unsettling, but it's only for a short time. I wish I could have left all this till tomorrow, but I wasn't sure how long it would take."

Nevertheless, the following morning when Lyn got up there was a home-made chocolate cake waiting for her, filled with butter cream, topped with a dusting of icing sugar, and with little blobs of butter cream all round its edge, each one topped with a brightly coloured Smartie.

"Will I be able to come and stay with you?" said Sue, when it was shared out at lunchtime.

"I don't know. I hope so."

"My mum says you can come and stay with us. Anyway, I'll write to you."

Lyn looked at her in sudden panic. "I don't know our new address," she said.

"It's all right," said Sue reassuringly. "My mum's got it, she said."

"We're not even going there yet," said Lyn. "We're going somewhere else first. And I don't think my dad even knows about it."

"Did you think he'd visit you there?"

"I'm not supposed to be seeing him till we're properly in the new flat. But I kept thinking he *might* look in down here, you know? I knew he wouldn't, but I thought he might. Knowing he positively can't is different."

Sue nodded. "Where is it you're going first?" she said.

"I don't know. A beach somewhere."

"What do you mean, a beach somewhere? Are you camping?"

"No, it's a house. A little house."

"What kind of house?"

"I don't know," said Lyn. "I don't know anything. When I'm grown up and I've got children, I shall tell them every single thing I'm going to do. I shall tell them everything till they're bored sick. They'll never have to go off to a house and not even know exactly where it is. I think I might run away and come back down and live with you, like cats and dogs do."

"I wish you would," said Sue.

"Well, I will," said Lyn. "If I don't like it."

Chapter Six

The bird had joined up with three or four others that were not quite of its kind, but similar. They were white, with the same crested heads and deeply forked tails, but they were smaller, and instead of the striking, vivid red their beaks were black, with yellow tips. However, their habits were the same, and they seemed to accept the newcomer without aggression. They all kept out to sea, feeding, waiting, rarely touching land.

The little house stood forlornly by itself, just off a road that was narrower than any Lyn had seen. It was dark when they arrived, and in fact it was this very darkness that told her how isolated it was. Where she came from, there were always lights. Even if she woke up and looked out of the window at two or three in the morning, there were lights. But here . . .

The lights had begun to grow scarcer almost as soon as they left the motorway. Eventually they had driven through a small, strung-out village. Then they were beyond the village, with the distinctive sound of the sea coming from their right, and a group of tiny houses, standing apparently in nothingness, on their left. Her mother stopped the hired car outside the last of these, and reached out a hand to prevent Lyn from undoing her seat belt. "Just going to collect the keys," she said.

She got out of the car, leaving the driver's door open, and ran the tiny distance to the front door of the little house. Into the drowsy warmth of the car's interior came fingers of chilly air with a peculiar smell. Lyn, who had been on holiday to the sea before, partly recognised it, but only partly – and then realised that that was because it was only part of a smell. The smell she had always associated with seaside holidays was made up of petrol fumes and salty air mixed with the rich sugariness of candy floss and dough-nuts and the vinegary greasiness of hot dogs and chips. Here, there was no mix, just one smell, sharp and thin, of salty water, salty wind. A stinging smell that didn't wrap around her in a welcoming way but seemed to prod at her and lick her curiously, as if it wondered what she was. She shivered, leant across the car and pulled the door shut against it.

Her mother, who had been talking to a stout old man with flaring white hair, outlined in his brightly lit doorway, turned at the sound. Then she said something more to him and ran back to the car, returning his wave as she got in. She started the engine and drove away from the little group of houses, not fast or far, to another small house, all on its own. Unlit of course; empty; its modest outline revealed by the headlights as the car turned off the road to park on a piece of sandy flatness, hemmed in by scratchy looking shrubs.

Lyn got out of the car and stood shivering in darkness. There were no stars, just the dim glow of the village in one direction, and a couple of tiny lights pin-pointing two other houses on the road far up ahead. She walked along the car and stood by the boot, holding on to it with one hand. She felt that if she didn't do this she might fall over. At first she assumed this was because of the long journey. Then she knew it was because of the extraordinary feeling of empti-ness all around her. She had often been aware of something standing nearby in darkness, but she had never before realised that it was possible to be so strongly aware of nothing.

Her mother left the headlights on until she had opened up the house and put on all its own lights – sitting room light, kitchen light, bathroom light, and the lights in the two tiny upstairs bedrooms. Only when she and Lyn had carried in all their possessions, in three or four trips, did she switch off the headlights and lock up the car for the night.

Inside, Lyn was suddenly so overcome with heaviness and sleepiness from the journey that it didn't occur to her to explore the house, or even to pay it very much attention. She saw only that it was as neat and pretty as a doll's house, and almost as unreal. It had the odd look of a house that is not actually a home. Everything was there that you would expect, yet it looked unfinished. There were two little armchairs, one on each side of a tiny empty grate, a square table with four little wooden chairs pushed in under it, a faded but clean carpet, a rug by the fireplace, a table with a lamp on it by each armchair. Over the mantelpiece, which had a stopped clock at its centre, hung a single picture; of a sailing ship being wrecked on rocks.

"Where are the people?" said Lyn blankly. She hadn't wondered until now.

"We're the people," said her mother. "It's a holiday cottage, didn't you realise? They rent it out, but no one wants it at the moment so we can have it free."

Lyn shook her head in wonderment and sat down in one of the small armchairs. She was so tired she could hardly be bothered to focus her eyes. She drank the soup her mother heated up, washed in cold water because the gas water heater refused to be lit, and went to bed in the doll's house bedroom in a haze of sleepiness.

In the morning they both slept late. "It's the sea air," said her mother, as she carried the poppy tray, laid with tea and toast, into the tiny living room. Wouldn't it be a surprise, Lyn thought, if the heat from the teapot ripened the painted seed heads and they shook little black poppy-eggs all over the tray. She began to try to explain the idea to her mother, as she set down the breakfast, but then they both noticed that three things had been dropped through the small letter box. Lyn stopped talking and went to pick them up; two postcards and a letter. She half expected them to be addressed to strangers, but they were not. The envelope was addressed to her mother, in her grandmother's handwriting, and both the postcards were for her, from Sue. "Look at this!" she said, and she could feel that her face was smiling by itself. "People know we're here!"

"Well, of course they do," said her mother, amused. "Did you think we'd done a flit?" She sat at the table and tore open her envelope.

Lyn sat down beside her and looked at the postcards. One was a picture of the Queen, looking regal in a white dress and blue sash. The other was of one of the Yeomen Warders of the Tower of London – the actual one, Lyn realised, that she and Sue had talked to on one of the school's days out.

"She must have posted these before we left," she said. "They must have been travelling up here at the same time as us – more or less."

"Gran sends you lots of love," said her mother. "We're going over for the day on Thursday."

Lyn turned over the picture of the Queen to read the message. "She misses you," it said.

"Nice thought!" said Lyn aloud.

"Yes," said her mother, still reading. "She's going to make brown bread ice cream."

"I doubt that," said Lyn. "I think she'd ask the Royal Chef." She read on: "Have you been talking of sea in geography without you seeing eroded earth pillars! they don't look good Write soon, love." She read it again more carefully. It still didn't seem to make sense and it wasn't even signed.

She put down the Queen and picked up the Beefeater. "The Queen says and so do I." She read, "swimming in the sea? I'm writing these on Friday afternoon, you're drawing BAD LUCK, MATE, from here. Sue."

She put the Beefeater down and looked at her mother. "Sue's gone off her head," she said.

Her mother folded away her own letter, poured a mug of tea for Lyn and set it beside the postcards. Then she tapped the nearest with her first finger. "Can I see?"

"Go ahead," said Lyn, passing them both, and then suddenly snatching them back – "No, wait, just a minute," she said. She laid the cards down side by side, next to the toast rack, where they could both see, aligning them carefully. "Got it," she said. "Read straight across."

"The Queen says she misses you and so do I," her mother read aloud. "Have you been swimming in the sea? Talking of sea, I'm writing these in geography on Friday afternoon, without you seeing. You're drawing eroded earth pillars! BAD LUCK, MATE, they don't look good from here. Write soon, love Sue."

"What's an eroded earth pillar?" said her mother.

"She must have posted these after school on Friday," said Lyn. "Doesn't post get here fast?"

"She *has* put first class stamps on them. We're not abroad, you know."

"Two first class stamps," said Lyn, admiring them. "That's true friendship, that is."

After breakfast her mother filled the tray again and carried it the few steps to the kitchen. "You're at the seaside," she said. "You'd better go out and explore."

"This isn't my idea of the seaside," said Lyn, going to stand at the living room window where she could look out on the cool, hazy day. She could see the narrow road outside the house and high sand dunes. Not much else.

"It's beside the sea," said her mother. "I don't know what else seaside is."

"It isn't like a holiday place, though, is it? There doesn't seem to be anything here."

"Why don't you go out and look around?"

Lyn thought for a moment. Then, "come with me," she said.

"Not just now. I want to put all our stuff away, I was too

tired last night. And I want to check what we need from the shops."

"I'll wait till you're ready, then," said Lyn. "I'll watch TV. Where is it?"

"There isn't one."

"No TV! Not anywhere? What are we going to do all the time?"

"We're only here for a few days – this is simply a stop gap."

"We've got to survive while we are here, though, haven't we?"

"Don't be silly. Go out and have a wander round. I couldn't get you in when we were in London, now we're by the sea and I can't get you out. You are an odd child."

"When do we go to the shops?"

"Later. I'll call you. Go on."

"But I don't think there's anything out there," said Lyn.

"Put on your anorak, it's quite cold."

Reluctantly, Lyn went out of the small house into the emptiness outside.

The sky was white and seemed low. It curved only slightly down towards the horizon. It was like a shallow lid; a shallow white enamelled lid. There was a white mist at the horizon and the beach vanished into this white mist at each end of its long dull curve. The mist came and went somewhat, now denser, now clearer, as the air moved it, but did not reveal anything different.

The dunes were pale brown, not yellow like sand but beige like sandpaper. Coarse grass grew on them in patches and it looked grey; and short, twisted, bristly bushes stood on them in small groups and they were grey, too.

It looked like a model landscape made by a child, and it seemed to Lyn that she herself might be a little model figure out of a packet, one of a set – of which the father had been lost and the mother put away indoors. She set her feet squarely on the road surface and didn't look down so that it was easy to pretend that her ankles disappeared into a little rectangular base on which she was balanced. She stuck her arms downward and stiffly outwards from her sides and stood still. She felt that if she could only remain perfectly still , like that, nothing would ever move or change again. The sky would never grow dark, nor would it ever grow sunny. She would not become older or taller, the sand would not slide down the dunes, the grass would not move in the breeze because there would be no breeze to move it.

But she was not able to put the vision to the test because there was a breeze, and it was cold, and she found that she could not bear to stand still in it. It cut. Its coldness cut her legs and her hands and her face. She walked a little way along the road, which was of grey tarmac salted with a fine covering of sand. Then she turned left on to the dunes and found that they were not static at all, but shifting. The sand gave way under her feet as she climbed, sometimes closing drily over them, sometimes just pouring heavily downwards beneath them, so that a second step did not carry her much further than a first. The tussocks of grass, even those too far away to be affected by her climbing feet, were some of them deeply embedded and some so exposed that their roots were just showing.

She reached the top of the dunes and looked along them, the sea to her left, the dunes curving ahead and to her right. From there it looked as though the shore was breaking in waves against the sea; the waves of sand always moving yet always the same, just like the waves of the sea.

She looked down at the firmer sand, between the base of the dunes and the water's edge, but even that was not really stable. The weight of the water at high tide had compacted it together to give an illusion of solidity – but this seemingly solid ground was ruffled into long narrow curving shapes, mirror images of the waves that had risen and fallen above it a few hours earlier. The massive dunes rose up and crashed down like breakers and sent ripples across the compacted sand to meet the ripples that swirled in from the sea breakers on the other side. It was as though the land was so strongly influenced by the nearness of the sea that it had begun to imitate it, and had almost forgotten that it was made of entirely different stuff.

And everywhere there was nothing. Nothing on the dunes but her. Nothing on the beach but a few birds on a flat outcrop of dingy rock, which barely rose above the level of the sand. Nothing on the sea but a few gulls, hardly moving because the swell was so slight.

She wouldn't admit, even to herself, that she was cold, but her ears hurt and she cupped her hands over them to try to protect them from the sharp air.

Everything, here, seemed to be sharp. The hard grains of sand in her shoes rubbed sharply against her feet, the greenish-grey dune grass flicked sharply across her legs, the voices of the calling birds came sharply out of their sharp beaks, and the cold that touched her face and hands, and the pain in her ears, were piercing. Her ears were so pointedly uncomfortable that it was as though someone had threaded a fine wire in at one, through her head and out at the other. She felt almost as though the spirit of the place could tighten this wire and lift her up by it, and hang her on some invisible line, out of its way.

Rubbish! she thought. I'm stronger than you, I can run and jump and kick your stupid sand all about, and pull up your grass, and dig up your beach, and do anything I want.

She locked her hands above her head – a high-speed train powered by an overhead cable – and ran along the tops of the dunes as fast as they would let her, giving out as loud a roar of electrical energy as she could manage. Up, down, up, along she went, following the rolling shapes of sand, till at a high point she caught one foot in an unyielding tussock of grass, skidded with the other, and sent a great pale shower of sand raining down into the deep hollow below. Even as she regained her footing and drew breath for the next high-speed charge, the figure of a man uncurled itself from the bottom of the hollow where it had been crouching and reared up towards her with a growling shout.

Lyn slithered, stopped herself, turned and ran – ran back over the dunes to the road – ran with her heart hammering so loudly in her chest and head and ears that she couldn't hear if she was followed or not.

Chapter Seven

In the safety of the space between the car and the house wall, Lyn gradually recovered herself. Her mother did not open the door, nor call out from inside, which reassured her that her ignominious flight had not been seen. She leant against the boot of the car and carefully scanned the landscape. She could only see the great barricade of dunes. She could not see the flat area that she could hardly bring herself to think of as a beach, nor could she see the sea itself.

There was no sign of the man. Nothing moved on the dunes, nothing looked disturbed or changed. She could not even pick out the tracks of her own flight – except where an extra skim of sand had been spread across the tarmac of the road as she had fled across it.

There was nowhere nearby that he could be hiding, no way that he could creep up on her without her seeing him when he was some way off. He must still be deep in amongst the dunes – perhaps in his same hollow.

Lyn bent forward to look at herself in the wing mirror of the car. If she looked too closely her face became distorted which made her feel uneasy. She pulled back a little. Now it just looked small and white – pinched – like Sharon's. She rubbed at her cheeks with the palms of her hands, to bring some colour to them, but they were so cold that the rubbing hurt her and all that happened was that her eyes watered and her nose began to redden. Even more like Sharon. She turned abruptly from the mirror – just because you began to look a bit like someone, that didn't mean you had to behave like them. She felt in need of action.

She knew perfectly well, of course, what you did when confronted by a strange man. She had been told often enough. You got yourself as far away as possible, as fast as possible, and pointed him out to the nearest trustworthy adult.

Even so, if this had happened on the Estate she'd have given him the run-around, found out what he was up to, where he was heading. Here, though, she felt at a loss, and not simply because the area was strange to her. It was the silence that made it so peculiar. It was not a complete silence. There was a faint restless noise from the sluggish sea, there were the random and distant cries of the birds, and there was the sharp cold-induced pain in her ears, which was almost like a sound in itself. But there seemed no specific sounds that she could learn to understand – like the distinctive clank of an individual lift or the particular echo of footsteps which signalled unmistakably the exact where-abouts of the feet that made them.

She decided to stay on the house side of the road and walk just a little way from it, parallel to the dunes, in the hope of finding a vantage point from which she could see him. She was already beginning to convince herself that she would feel much safer when she knew exactly where he was. There was no high ground this side of the road, she could see that from where she stood, but she had noticed that some of the larger dunes lay diagonally between road and beach and she thought it might be possible to get a useful view in amongst them, from the correct angle, and at a discreet distance.

Walking was much easier away from the sliding sand, and because of this she found she couldn't judge how far along the dunes she had travelled before. There didn't seem to be any landmarks. On this side of the road the ground underfoot was a dreary sandy-earthy mixture with thin grass in patches and clusters of prickly-looking weeds lying flat to the ground. At intervals along the road's edge were clumps of grey-leaved uninteresting-looking bushes with twisted woody stems and fierce spikey twigs. At her approach, one or two sparrow-like birds sprang off the topmost twigs of the nearest one and flew away inland, dipping over the murky ground as if they couldn't quite decide whether to keep going or land.

"Stupid things," said Lyn irritably. "What do you think I'm going to do to you anyway?"

Veering away from the scratchy threat of the bushes, and avoiding the worst of the prickly looking weeds, some of whose spines looked strong enough to pierce a shoe, Lyn moved farther in, away from the road, than she realised. She noticed that the ground was beginning to get damp and it struck her as typical of the unreasonableness of the place that it should get wetter the farther you got from the sea.

Even as she thought that, the dampness became more pronounced and as she began to cross some reddish brown grass, much thinner and more pointed than the flat blades on the dunes, she found she was sinking into sticky black mush. Instinctively, she ran. Though the mush seized her left shoe and tried to pull it off, she snatched her foot free, still shod, ran across the arm of tell-tale reddish grass which curved in front of her, and reached dry land. She crouched down and tried to tear off a handful of grass to wipe the worst of the mud off the side of her shoe, but the stems were so strong and wiry they threatened to cut her hands. So she managed to use the tufts as a kind of duster without detaching them from their roots.

Looking round she realised she must be well past the point in the dunes where he had been hiding. It was by now quite obvious that there were no vantage points on this side. All she could hope to see was someone who chose to walk along the crests. For something so bland and uninteresting the dune system seemed extraordinarily complicated. She decided to cross the road and work her way silently back along it, and to come upon him from the other side. But before she reached the road she felt her toe catch on something hard and unyielding and, unable to stop herself, fell forwards on to her hands and knees, her right hand firmly planted on one of the prickle-weeds.

"This rotten place," said Lyn furiously, crouching back on her heels and picking one or two fine silvery spines out of her palm. "It hates me."

She turned herself around, still crouching, to see what it was she had tripped over. It was a longish, straightish piece of metal, seemingly a dark silvery colour originally, but now tarnished and rusty. It looked familiar, but Lyn couldn't believe it was what it seemed to be. She bunny-hopped over it and felt around in the short miserable grass a little way from it. There she found an identical one, lying parallel to the first; the tracks of a narrow-gauge railway, or part of them. She stood up. Now that she knew where to look she could pick out where the track ran, or what was left of it. Along a very slightly raised strip of ground, built up – as she could see when she scuffed her foot between the rails and between the rotting remains of the sleepers that had joined them – of gravel from somewhere or other. It ran beside the road, far enough in from it to clear the backs of the tiny holiday house and of the group of houses where the old man with the flaring white hair had stood in his doorway. But not so far back from the road that it was endangered by the black, mushy ground, its ginger grass standing up in spikes like hair. A railway. A little old dead railway.

Lyn thought of the bright tracks that passed under the bridge near school; of all the activity, especially in the early evening; of the clattering trains with their sighing doors and of the surges of people, sucked in to them and expelled out from them, in noisy tides. She could have cried.

There had been life here once, it seemed. Only she was about a hundred years too late for it; or even a thousand, maybe. Her idea of history was very vague. She kicked the skeletal rails and, turning her back on them, crossed the road. No point in mourning them now.

She climbed and scrambled up among the dunes, wondering if it would ever be possible to learn their shapes, to recognise the tufts of grass and the angles of the sand slopes as easily as she could recognise the towers and walkways of the Estate. Or if, as soon as she got to know her way around, the wind would shift and rebuild everything into a new landscape that was once again unknown.

She had no idea where the man had been. It now seemed pointless to look for him. He could be anywhere. Even a tall man standing upright would be out of sight if he was in one of the sandy valleys. She stood for a moment, holding her aching ears and looking irritably at the empty sea. Sea should have pedalos or yachts, fishing boats, ferries, the heads of swimmers, something, anything. This had nothing. Just birds bobbing, birds standing in the shallows, birds pecking pointlessly at the flattish dark rocks to the right . . . She dropped her hands to her sides. The sea hissed distantly at her.

"Hallo," said a voice.

Lyn turned so sharply that she nearly fell over. The man was standing behind her, on a dune top, outlined blackly against the sky.

And that was when she realised how extraordinarily stupid she had been. By coming round behind him, she had placed him between her and home.

He was about the same age as her father. He wore brown corduroy trousers, a brown jumper, a dingy khaki anorak, big, hanging open, pockets all over its outside, pockets visible even in its lining.

"Hallo," he said again. He stood quite still.

Lyn didn't answer. In her mind she could picture a report in a newspaper. *A man in brown corduroy trousers, a brown jumper and an anorak was seen near the spot where the girl disappeared.* But who would have seen him? There was no one else here.

"It was you before, wasn't it?" said the man.

Lyn, still silent, began to edge very, very slowly side-ways, towards the road, to give herself a clear run.

"I'm sorry if I frightened you," he said. "To be honest, you frightened me. You can't hear much from the bottom of the dunes, so suddenly there was this great shriek and then a cloud of sand shot down all over me. I thought I was being attacked." He laughed as though he hoped she'd join in. He didn't seem to have noticed her slow-motion edging away. She kept on going, weight on the right foot, sliding the left foot, weight on the left foot, sliding the right foot. She didn't want to start running until she had to. The house was too far away. She knew she wouldn't be able to beat him to it from here.

"I was bird-watching," said the man. "With these." He put his hands into one of the deep outer pockets of the anorak and took out something which he held out on his hand, held out towards her. "Binoculars," he went on. "They're quite powerful. Would you like to have a go?"

He was too far away for her to see what it was that lay on his hand, but she knew it couldn't be binoculars. Sue's mother had some and she and Sue had borrowed them and gone to spy on the world from the top floor of Merrick Tower. They were big and heavy – they wouldn't lie on the palm of someone's hand, not even a man's hand, he would have to hold on to them properly.

She began to move, still crab-wise, a little faster. He stood where he was, but still held out his hand with the black object covering it.

Lyn worked her way around him – keeping a good distance between them – her eyes upon him all the time. He made no attempt to move towards her. When she had positioned herself so that there was a clear run across the dunes to the road, she made a dash for it, skittering across the surface of the sliding sand the way a waterboatman skitters across the shifting ripples of its pond. Once on the easier surface of the road, she ran full tilt back towards the house. She'd been stupid, she knew, very stupid, but she'd got away with it this time. Never again, she thought, in time with the pounding of her feet on the road. Never, never, never, never again.

She slowed to a more decorous pace as she realised that the old man, his flaring white hair somewhat quenched by what Sue would call a pully-woollon hat, was stumping past the little house, his back to her, accompanied by a Labrador so fat that its legs were pushed outwards by its girth, and it had to rock from side to side as it walked in order that its feet should touch the ground. Neither looked back and saw her, as they waddled off for their morning constitutional. And Lyn chose not to look behind her along the dunes. Twice, now, she had run in panic along more or less the same route. Enough was enough. The dunes could keep their horrors. She'd had it, she would stay indoors and paint – or go with her mother to the shops – and leave the great outdoors to its own mysterious devices.

She wandered casually into the little house, hung around a bit until her breathing was normal again, and then leant over her mother's shoulder to read the shopping list she was composing. Shops meant people and traffic and bustle and all the things she understood. Shopping, which she had once thought of as rather boring, was beginning to look as though it might be the highlight of each day.

Chapter Eight

Lyn fetched the shopping basket, which she had noticed hanging on the back of the kitchen door, and set it on the table beside the shopping list.

"You don't have to come with me," said her mother, not looking up, checking over the items she'd noted down.

"I'll come," said Lyn.

"You can play on the beach, if you'd rather."

"Play!" said Lyn. "There's no one to play with. Apart from that man."

Her mother looked up. "What man?"

Suddenly embarrassed, Lyn didn't know how to explain. "Oh, just some man," she said.

"What kind of man? What was he doing?"

"Oh I don't know. Sort of hiding. Then he came up behind me."

Her mother stood up, bumping the little dining chair back across the carpet. "Lyn! What have you always been told. . . ?"

"I know!" said Lyn. "I know! I didn't speak to him. I didn't go near him, I came straight back. What more could I do?"

Her mother stretched out one hand and touched her hair gently. "I'm sorry," she said. "You did absolutely right. But it does sound very odd. Did he say anything to you?"

"He said did I want to look through his binoculars. But they didn't look like any binoculars I've ever seen."

"What did they look like?"

"I didn't go close enough to see. It was black like binoculars, but too small. I expect it was just something he happened to have in his pocket. I expect he thought binoculars sounded interesting.'' Lyn found she was getting more nervous as she spoke. There had, after all, been that moment when he was between her and the house. And her mother was obviously shaken.

"I really didn't think there'd be anything like this out here," she said. "All that time in London I've been frightened for you, for nothing, and now, somewhere like this . . . "

"It's all right, though," said Lyn. "I'm back, unscathed." It was a word her father had used often. She had never been quite sure what happened to you if things went wrong and you were scathed. It somehow sounded like something that might take your skin off.

Her mother was zipping herself into her red anorak.

"Right," she said. "Show me whereabouts he is. I'll see if I can get a look at him, and then as soon as we get into the village, I'm going to tell the police."

She picked up the shopping basket and her purse and shunted Lyn out of the front door ahead of her. As soon as she'd locked it, she took Lyn's hand, holding it tightly, almost as though she was afraid her daughter might make a break for it and run away.

Lyn, who could see the old man and old dog plodding back from their walk, tried to pull her hand free. She felt far too old to have it held anyway, and certainly didn't want it held in public. But her mother, who had also seen the laboured approach, clung on firmly, and waited where she was.

"Hallo, Mr Parker," she called, as soon as he was within reasonable earshot.

"We cover a fair distance, you know," said Mr Parker, without preamble. "I don't know how we do it when we're both so overweight, but somehow we just keep going. There's nothing really to stop you, when it's all on the flat, I suppose."

As they both paused, the dog leant slightly against the

man's legs. Lyn watched, fascinated. It seemed to her that if Mr Parker moved off unexpectedly, the dog would be tipped over sideways by its own weight.

"Have you seen a man around here?" her mother was saying. "Behaving rather oddly?"

Mr Parker looked concerned. "No," he said. "Why? Has there been some trouble."

"Not exactly. But Lyn was in the dunes, over there, and a man came up and spoke to her. On the face of it, it was all quite straightforward, but I didn't like the sound of it."

Mr Parker's face cleared. "Youngish man?" he said to Lyn. "Brown cords? Khaki anorak?"

Lyn nodded. She was concentrating on trying to work her fingers free of her mother's grasp.

"Bill Walker," said Mr Parker. "Oh, nothing to worry about there, nothing at all. Teaches computer science. Comes up from time to time for the bird-watching. Staying with us, as it happens." He looked at Lyn and laughed in a kindly way. "Did he frighten you?" he said.

"No," said Lyn stoutly. "I frightened him."

"I expect you did, too," said Mr Parker, "if you came up on him suddenly. He gets very carried away. Forgets there's anyone else in the world." He set off across the road towards the dunes calling, "Bill, hey Bill, let's be having you." The dog waddled rather unenthusiastically with him, its head down, trying to snort some sand out of its nostrils.

Although the shouts seemed to disperse into the empty, misty air, they did draw a response, and the figure of the man rose from the dunes and began to lope towards them. The dog gave an immense honking cough and then sat down, apparently satisfied.

"Sorry," said Mr Parker across the narrow road. "Old dogs do make the most disgusting noises."

The arrival of Bill Walker, not looking at all strange now that he had been pronounced to be normal, put paid to the idea of shopping for that morning. By the time the introductions had been completed they were all, even the old sniffly dog, inside, sitting around the tiny dining table, while Lyn's mother made coffee, out of sight though not out of earshot in the kitchen.

Bill Walker was very apologetic when he was told about the trouble he had caused. "I shouldn't have followed you," he said to Lyn. "I should have had more sense. I thought I'd frightened you before, and I wanted to reassure you, but of course that wasn't the way to do it. Very stupid of me. I'm sorry."

"She tells me she wasn't frightened," said Mr Parker.

"You ran fast," said Bill Walker to Lyn.

"You growled at me from your sandpit."

"That," said Bill, "was a scream of fear."

"More like a roar," said Lyn.

"I grant you it may have been a macho sort of scream, but it *was* fear. It's usually quite empty out there at this time of year, apart from the birds."

"I am a bird."

"The sort I watch have smaller feet."

Lyn's mother set three cups of coffee and a glass of milk on the table. Lyn made a face at the milk. She didn't much like coffee, but today she would have liked to drink what everyone else was drinking.

"Lyn, fetch the plate of biscuits, would you?" said her mother. "They wouldn't fit on the tray."

As she turned in at the kitchen, Lyn heard Bill say, "Is the water heater behaving?"

"No, since you ask," said her mother. "I haven't been able to persuade the pilot light to stay lit."

"It's a knack," said Bill, getting up. "Do you mind if I do it for you?"

"I wish you would."

"I'll show Lyn how, while she's out here," said Bill, fitting himself into the small kitchen. "Once you know the trick you can't fail."

Lyn set down the plate she'd just picked up and turned with interest to the sink water heater, which was designed to supply the adjoining lean-to bathroom as well. But her mother followed Bill out, put the biscuit plate back into her hand and pushed her gently towards the sitting room. "I think gas heaters are best left to grown-ups," she said.

Lyn shrugged and retired to the sitting room to eat chocolate finger biscuits with Mr Parker.

"Is it all right to give one to him?" she said, looking down at the black mass of sleeping dog at the old man's feet.

"Well ..." Mr Parker looked dubious. "Best not indoors," he said at last. "His teeth aren't what they were and he tends to suck biscuits rather than chew them. Doesn't do a lot for the carpet. Not that the Moores would mind, but your mother might feel responsible. Do you know the Moores?"

"I don't think so," said Lyn.

The water heater having been persuaded to become operational, Bill returned to the table and his coffee.

"I think you met Pam once," said her mother, following him, "when she came to London. We'll see more of them now, though."

"Are they coming here?" said Lyn. "There isn't much room."

"Of course not," said her mother, laughing. "They only come down once a year. But when we move into the new flat we won't be far away from their house."

"I've known them on and off for twenty years," said Mr Parker dreamily. "And Bill here's known 'em for about six."

"Do you usually rent this cottage?" said Lyn's mother, suddenly, anxiously, to Bill. "Is that how you know about the heater? Have we forced you out?"

"Not at all. I usually come a bit later in the spring and again in the autumn. This was an unplanned trip, due to ..."

He glanced at Mr Parker as he spoke and it seemed to Lyn

that an odd expression came on to Mr Parker's face. It was only there briefly, and she couldn't really have described it, but Bill seemed to see it, too, because he stopped in midsentence and then turned back to her mother. "No, you had the prior claim," he said. "And I'm very comfortable with the Parkers."

"We like the company," said Mr Parker.

Lyn's mother, still looking bothered, began to say, "Oh I do hope . . ." But Bill had taken the binoculars out of his pocket – they really were binoculars, Lyn now saw, but folding ones and the smallest she had ever encountered – and was offering them to her, and Mr Parker was at the same time asking her where they both came from.

"London," said Lyn, taking the glasses and going to the window with them.

"Do be careful with those," said her mother. "Don't drop them."

"She won't drop them," said Bill calmly. "Do you see where to adjust the focus?"

"Yes, thank you." They were indeed powerful. They brought a bunch of spiky grass on the dune-top over the road so close that when a breeze moved it she drew back a little, half expecting to feel it scratch her face. "We lived near an Estate," she said, searching for something to look at other than the grass, "with six towers and walkways and lifts and everything. All the towers had names – one of them was called Parker."

"There now," said Mr Parker. "So the London branch of the family made their mark."

"We actually lived in quite a nice flat in quite a nice residential road," said her mother. "But all she cared about was this wretched rough Estate. She's even painted it. Lyn, go and get your picture and see if anyone else thinks that awful place is as lovely as you seem to . . ."

"It's still packed," said Lyn.

"Well, unpack it."

"I will later," said Lyn, who had no wish to show off her most recent effort, which she had kept as a memento even though she suspected it of being worse than the one she had shredded with such rage. "I'll show it later. Mr Parker, do you mean the tower's really named after your family?"

"Sadly, I think probably not. Unless all the Parkers sprang from the same root hundreds of years ago. How are you getting on with those glasses?"

"They're terrific. It's just a shame there's nothing to look at through them."

"You can have a go with them outside later on," said Bill.

"There's nothing to look at out there, either," said Lyn, lowering the binoculars, and then handing them reluctantly back.

Bill laughed, but Mr Parker looked almost shocked for a moment.

"You *are* joking?" said Bill.

"I'm not. I've been out there. It's totally empty. It's an *awful* place . . ."

"Lyn, don't be so rude," said her mother.

"I'm not. I'm just saying. There's nothing there."

"There are a few birds," said Bill.

"Well, but they all look the same, and they're not interesting anyway."

"If you paint pictures," said Bill, "you must be more observant than you're letting on."

"Not good pictures."

"Even so. Do you truly think all those birds out there are identical?" He didn't ask as though he was trying to catch her out, he asked as though he was interested in her answer. So it seemed only fair to give him a considered one. After a moment of thought, Lyn said, "No, not all."

"Aha," said Bill.

"There are two kinds," said Lyn. "There are little brown sparrow things on the bushes, that flit away when you get near. And down by the sea there are gulls."

"Gulls?"

"Seagulls." She began to laugh. "White screaming things," she said. "You can't miss them."

They were all laughing now, even her mother, although she looked as though she wasn't quite sure why.

"Come for a walk with me, soon," said Bill. "And let me see if I and the binoculars can persuade you there's more than one kind of white screaming thing. That's if your mother doesn't mind?"

"No, it's very kind of you. But I wouldn't want her to be a nuisance to you."

"Not at all," said Bill. "This is a challenge. What about this afternoon?"

"That's fine by me," said Lyn's mother.

"Lyn?" said Bill. "We could walk along the beach and have a look at the castle and I could perhaps point out one or two things on the way."

"Castle?" said Lyn. "There's no *castle*. You're pulling my leg."

Bill buried his face in his hands. "You haven't even noticed the castle?" he said. He dropped his hands and shook his head in exaggerated sorrow. "What kind of paintings do you do, exactly?"

"Now be fair on the child," said Mr Parker, heaving himself to his feet. "The mist's been very thick this morning. Buster and I couldn't see the castle, and we know it's there. I think we should be moving. May will be wanting a hand with the potatoes."

"I'll drop by about two-thirty, then, if that's all right," said Bill.

"Yes, that's all right," said Lyn. It might not be quite as good as Sue dropping by to fetch her to watch the rush hour trains, but it was not bad. Really not bad at all.

Chapter Nine

The castle made Lyn furious.

By early afternoon the breeze had cleared the mist away, and by the time she and Bill set out to walk towards it, it was so clearly visible that she could understand his amazement that she had not noticed it earlier. However, when they reached it, it turned out to be very disappointing.

It was true that it stood on top of a modest cliff which made a break in the long sweep of dunes and beach; and that though the cliff wasn't high the castle did dominate its surroundings in quite a dramatic way; and that from its ramparts the sea did seem quite a long way down. But it was severely ruined, far worse than it had looked from a distance. The broken ramparts protected nothing more than a spaced-out arrangement of ruins, mostly two-foot high walls, enclosing nothing, where once had been rooms. The massive keep which, apart from the ramparts, was the only substantial remnant, had lost its middle floor and roof so that once through the doorless doorway there was nothing to see but smooth darkish walls, with the occasional hole for a beam or a window, rising up towards open sky.

It was all extremely tidy. There was no rubble; though most of the structure had clearly fallen, it was not lying around in chunks, it had all been tidied away somewhere. The ruins stood around politely on perfectly trimmed lawns which ran right up to the edges of their broken walls, making it look almost as though the whole thing had been built that way on purpose.

Lyn could not imagine what it had been like when it was whole, yet it reminded her of something. Unreasonable though it might seem, it reminded her – with its enclosing walls on which the remains of a walkway could be seen and with its solid-looking central keep – of the Estate. It was like a derelict image of it, it was how the Estate might look to visitors centuries into the future, after some terrible war or long neglect – like it, yet totally different. Large and imposing – but open to the sky. At least one huge tower – but hollow, no stairs, no lifts, not even any floors. And silent. She thought of all the sounds on the Estate – clanking of lifts, banging of doors, shouting and calls, running feet, that strange wailing sound that Sharon had feared was ghosts. If any of those sounds were heard here, they would indeed be made by ghosts. The doors that banged would be heavy and wooden, the clanking would be made by the chains that raised the portcullis, the feet would be in no shoes that she had ever seen, and the wailing . . . If that kind of desperate crying was ever heard here it would come from people locked in a dungeon below ground whose release would not be effected by the simple pressing of a button.

And if this was like a long-dead image of the Estate, those rusty little broken rails half-hidden in scrubby grass were like a long-dead image of the busy tracks under the bridge near school.

It was a creepy idea and she didn't like it. She wished she could share it with Sue. If this place sold anything so frivolous as postcards, which clearly it didn't, she would have sent her one, and on it written – Dear Sue, This is a dead land, Love Lyn.

A Herring Gull shrieked overhead.

P.S., she thought, with its own vultures.

"What do you think?" asked Bill unwisely.

"I think it's dead and empty, just like everything else here."

"I think I'm sorry I asked," said Bill.

"The walk here was nice, though," Lyn said, pulling herself together. "Really nice."

It had been, too.

He had led her in among the dunes, showing her how they formed natural hides from which it was easy to watch the birds on the shore and in the shallows without frightening them. He had talked easily, most of the time, about himself, about the birds, about the best binoculars. He had shown her how to lie on her stomach, propping herself on her elbows, so that the birds would not be disturbed by small movements and she would be able to hold the binoculars steady.

"But why do you want to watch them?" Lyn had said. "Why is it so great to be able to recognise them?"

"I don't know," Bill had said. He had handed her the binoculars. "Now look straight ahead," he had said, "along the line of that breakwater. You should be able to get three of your 'white screaming things' in your sights. Look carefully. Are they all exactly the same? Same size, same colour of wings, of heads, of legs?"

At first, inexperienced in the use of binoculars, Lyn had seen nothing but sky, then nothing but sand. Then she had caught the edge of the breakwater and the three birds. She had found she had to swing the glasses very slightly from left to right to get them all in, they weren't very close to each other and one was already walking off.

"Well?"

"No, they're not," Lyn had said. They were all what she would have called seagulls but, to her surprise, there were distinct differences. "The one on the left's bigger and it's got pink legs. The one in the middle hasn't got such a ferocious beak and it's got yellow legs. These binocs *are* good! And the one – oh – the one that's just flown off, that was smaller still, and quite light coloured, and its head was dirty, not white like the others. And it had red legs."

"Excellent! You've spotted three different birds."

Lyn had known that she was grinning as she had passed back the glasses. "I have?" she'd said.

"All right . . . so what was so great about spotting them?"
Lyn had laughed. "I don't know either," she'd agreed.

"The largest one is a Herring Gull. You must have seen
them before. Even if not at the seaside. They often go into
town and feed on rubbish tips and so on. The smaller one
with the yellow legs is a Common Gull. Though actually it's
not as common as the Herring Gull. And the one that got
away – which is bobbing about on the sea over there – here,
try and get it in the glasses – is a Black-Headed Gull."

"No, it wasn't black, it was dirty grey."

"They only put on their black hoods in summer. In fact,
strictly they're dark brown, not black, but don't worry about
that for now. But they never go totally white, even in
winter."

"Got it! And there's another one sitting on the sea just
beside it. It's got a black smudge, kind of behind its eye, as
though someone with dirty fingers picked it up by its head."

"That's it. That'll grow into a dark hood later on. There
are actually four or five more sitting out there on the water, if
you can find them."

When they'd done with the Black-Headed Gulls, they
watched a diver for a while – a Red-Throated Diver, Bill had
guessed, though it was too far away to see clearly and he
admitted it probably hadn't grown its summer red throat
yet. He had said it was working its way north, to its breeding
grounds in Scotland. Lyn had felt quite worn out watching
it. It would cruise on top of the water quite calmly for a while
and then suddenly fling itself into a half-somersault and dis-
appear beneath it. By the time it surfaced the first time, she
had already convinced herself it had drowned. And even
when she got used to its protracted disappearances she
found she could not guess where it would pop up next. It
was best, Bill had said, to watch with the naked eye and
bring up the binoculars only when it reappeared. The first
time, she had been so eager she had nearly blacked both her
eyes.

Eventually, Bill had said he didn't want to dazzle her with too many birds all at once, so they'd left their sandy hiding place and walked the rest of the way to the castle along the tops of the dunes, Lyn complaining about the sharp lashing the coarse grass gave to her legs. However, when Bill had said it was mostly Marram Grass which served a useful purpose by holding the dunes in place, Lyn had looked at it more carefully.

"But they still shift around?" she had said, as an ill-judged step sent a small avalanche down into one of the smaller hollows.

"Oh yes, but not so much. It's the network of roots, you see. Hangs on to it all, a bit like a hairnet."

"I think I need some Marram Grass in my life," Lyn had said. "To keep it all in place."

"What a very unadventurous attitude, if I may say so. Life is all about change."

"You can have too much of it," Lyn had said, adding that although she now saw its purpose she felt it was probably easier to love Marram Grass if you were wearing corduroy trousers than if you were wearing a skirt and short socks, and that tomorrow she would wear her jeans.

Now – hanging over the castle wall – she said, "It's not up to much as a castle, but it is a good viewpoint."

"Especially a bit later in the year," said Bill. "It's still winter as far as most birds are concerned, though very late winter. Soon they'll think about nesting – more birds will arrive – far more. There'll be nests on the cliff below the castle on the other side, and the castle walls are a terrific place to watch them from. And the Terns'll come and nest on the beach, and this is one of the best places to watch them from, with good binoculars."

"Turns?" said Lyn. "What kind of turns? Funny turns? Three point turns?"

"Sandwich Terns, mostly."

She stared at him.

"Truly," he said.

Lyn hung herself on the wall, the way she and Sue used to hang themselves on the bridge wall over the railway tracks, the toes of her shoes scuffing at the ancient stones. Bill turned his back to the wall, the way Sue so often had, and leant on it with his elbows, looking up at the sky with his eyes screwed up.

"All those little sparrow sort of birds," said Lyn. "Were they all different sorts, too?"

"I expect so. Might have been linnets, or greenfinches, or yellowhammers. We can have a look at that side another time. There's a bit of salt marsh the other side of the road that leads back into a rough heathland. You get quite a lot of interesting stuff there – especially when the spring migration really begins."

"This bird-watching," said Lyn, "isn't as straightforward as it might be, is it? I mean, according to you, the Common Gull isn't common, and the Black-Headed Gull doesn't have a black head."

"In winter, it doesn't."

"And in summer it's brown anyway."

"Oh, you haven't begun to grasp the problems," said Bill. He hitched himself up until he was sitting on the broken wall, his back to the drop which swept down to the thin line of road below, his heels hitting the stonework more or less in time with her toes. "There's not only summer plumage and winter plumage – and the species where the male and female are different – there's the juveniles to sort out, too." He struck his forehead with his hand. "Oh, the juveniles!"

"They dress differently again, do they?"

"Not half."

"What – punk hairdos and safety pins through their beaks?"

"I wish they did. That would help a lot. The immature gulls, for instance, all tend to be speckly brown and hideously alike."

"Don't they stick with their families? Can't you just look at the grown-ups?"

"Very intelligent suggestion, that. But the families tend to get all mixed up, especially in winter when they're not competing for nesting sites. It's a brave ornithologist who tries to tell the difference between a Great Black-Backed Gull in its first winter and a Herring Gull in its second winter."

"I'm going off this," said Lyn.

"No, no, don't do that. Take no notice of me. There are lots of easy ones. You don't need to worry about the tricky ones for years, if ever."

"Wow!" said Lyn. "A car coming down the road. This place is really waking up."

Bill turned idly round to watch the small grey Ford as it puttered extremely slowly northwards, in the direction of the little house. "Rats!" he said unexpectedly, and with some feeling.

"What's the matter?"

"Oh nothing. Just someone I'd rather not see up here, that's all."

The car pulled carefully off the road on the landward side, and stopped. A woman got out. Even without the binoculars, Lyn could see she was elderly with short, curly grey hair. She had binoculars of her own and, locking the car, she paced across the road and made her way laboriously to the top of a sand dune where she raised her glasses to her eyes and began to sweep them slowly across the beach.

Lyn was hardly aware of a movement beside her, but when she looked round Bill was not there, he was some way off across the smooth grass, examining the tidily shattered wall of the castle keep. Lyn, with all her experience of dodging gangs around the Estate, could see exactly what he'd done. He'd got himself as far away from any of the outer walls as possible, so that not even the best binoculars could spy him out.

The woman stood almost completely still, turning her head so slowly it was hardly like a movement at all, as she conducted her careful survey of the beach. Bill fussed and fidgeted around the keep walls, touching here, tapping with the toe of his shoe there, clearly bored. Lyn stood and watched them both, one small, calm and far below, the other large, near and irritable.

"Is she looking for you?" she said at last.

"Oh no," said Bill. "She doesn't know I'm here, and I don't want her to. Can you see her from there?"

"Yes."

"Will you tell me if she goes away?"

"OK. What'll we do if she doesn't?"

He shrugged. "You can go back whenever you want, of course," he said. "But if you don't mind, I'll try and lie low until the coast's clear." He laughed. "Literally!" he said.

"Who is she?" said Lyn.

"She's a dreadful woman."

"It's quite all right," said Lyn sharply. "No one ever tells me anything, I'm quite used to it."

Bill looked quickly over at her and Lyn realised she had surprised them both with her outburst. She felt suddenly embarrassed – this might be something private that she shouldn't know about. To fill up any possibly awkward pauses, she kept talking. "My mother, for example, never tells me anything at all. It must be something about me because other people's parents tell them things. Even when it's something that affects me, I don't get told. It's just 'We're off now – oh, didn't you realise – wasn't it obvious?'…"

"Do you tell people things?" said Bill, interrupting her.

"What?"

"Well, for example, do you tell your mother everything that happens at school, everything you do when you're away from her?"

"She wouldn't be interested."

"Do you tell her anything? You haven't told me anything. I've told you where I live, where I work, how often I come up here, when I first started bird-watching. You haven't told me anything at all. It is supposed to be two-way, you know."

Lyn was taken aback. "Well what do you want to know?" she said.

"Anything. What life was like in London would do. But first, is that awful woman still there?"

"She's going back to her car."

"Good. Just tell me when she drives off."

She did, but very slowly, and not far. Then she parked and made her way to the top of another dune, where she stood statue-like once more, the binoculars up to her eyes.

Bill sat down on the grass, his back to the keep wall, his legs stretched out in front of him. "I'm a prisoner," he said pathetically. "Entertain me."

So, leaning on the castle wall, like a sentry at ease, she told him all she could think of – about the Estate, school, Sue, Mandy, Sharon and her home-sickness, the trains, the secrets of the stuck lifts and, after a small pause, about her father and the half-brother. It was the most she'd ever talked to one person at one time. Once, she stopped completely and just stared out over the ramparts, unmoving. "Go on," Bill said. But she didn't, not at once. The grey-haired woman, who had scanned the cliffs below the castle thoroughly, had all at once turned her binoculars on to its rough walls, and for an uneasy minute Lyn knew she must be in her sights. It was an odd feeling, even though she knew the woman could have no interest in her whatever.

"I thought she shouldn't see that I was talking to someone," she said to Bill when the binoculars were once more directed out to sea. "You'd make a good spy," said Bill admiringly. "You'll be able to teach your half-brother a thing or two."

"I doubt it," said Lyn. "I've got awkward, so my dad's starting again with a new one."

"Most people who have children," said Bill, "have more than one. Do you think they all have the second one because they're sick of the first?"

"But he's gone away to have this one," said Lyn.

"No, I think you'll find he went away for other reasons. And because he liked having you around he decided he wanted another one."

"Then he won't want me any more, will he?"

"I meant another one as well, not instead. You do realise, don't you, that he may think you don't care about him any more. When you next see him he may want you to reassure him that you still do."

"It all seems very complicated," said Lyn.

"Oh it is," said Bill. "Yes, it is. What is that unlovely woman doing?"

"Believe it or not, she's going back to her car. But don't get excited yet, she didn't go far last time."

This time, though, she drove the little grey car on along the road, maddeningly slowly, but without stopping again. Lyn watched until the car was out of sight.

"All clear," she said. "This time it's definitely all clear."

"What a relief," said Bill. "I'm hungry."

Together they made their way back towards their respective temporary homes, their respective teas.

"My turn to give information," said Bill, as they went. "No big deal. She's an ornithologist. She also happens to be one of my least favourite people in the world."

"Why?"

"Oh, some ornithologists are dreadful people, especially in pursuit of the rare. She once told me she'd watched a Yellowlegs for five hours on a Welsh beach from a few yards away. It's a kind of Sandpiper…"

"Sandpiper?"

"It comes from North America and it's very rare to see

one over here. It was clearly exhausted, but because of its rarity she watched it, she photographed it, she was swollen with pride. She stayed there till it died. Now if she'd gone away and left it in peace to preen and rest without her beady eye on it, it just might have recovered."

"Poor old bird," said Lyn. She tried one of her sideways skips and almost fell down an unexpected dip. "Are you afraid that if she sees you she'll stare at you till you die?"

He laughed. "No. I'm just lazy. I couldn't be bothered to have a conversation with her. Also, if she saw me here, not at my usual time, she might assume I had inside information about something special and decide to stick around. As it is, with luck she'll go farther up the coast."

"I hope you didn't mind telling me about her," said Lyn.

"Not at all. Didn't hurt a bit. Did you mind telling me your life story?"

"No."

They walked on in silence for a bit. Then Lyn said, "I only want to be told reasonable things, you know. Things that affect me. Things that are my business."

"Sure."

"I mean—I think you are up here for a special reason. I think it's a secret. And I think Mr Parker's in on it." She watched his face. His expression did not change. "But that isn't my business and I don't expect to be told things like that."

"Well that's fair enough, then," said Bill.

Lyn, who had meant what she had said, did not even realise she had been fishing for information until she saw that none was going to be forthcoming.

That evening she spent some time sitting alone on top of the dune immediately opposite the house, looking vaguely around for anything unusual, at the same time knowing perfectly well that she wouldn't know it if she saw it. She counted two Herring Gulls and three Black-Headed Gulls, but saw nothing spectacular; no eagle, no vulture, no ornithologists. I shall probably never know, she thought. Rats!

Chapter Ten

The next morning, Lyn wanted to go out and look for Bill at once, but her mother said she mustn't make a nuisance of herself and kept her firmly indoors, even when the pale sea mist dispersed and a cool sun brought a dull glitter to the big dunes opposite.

So she got out the little cardboard writing case her grandmother had given her for Christmas, with the leaves of different coloured writing paper tucked in at one side and the different coloured envelopes tucked in at the other, and read through the letter to Sue she had begun the evening before.

"Dear Sue," she read, "Your postcards were great. I'll tell you what there isn't here – since we got to this house I haven't seen a shop, a café, or a bus. There's no pier or anything on the beach. I'm not sure there's a 'me'. I think I may be turning into Sharon. Also there's no noise."

She had written that bit before going to bed the night before, but it was not until she was actually in bed that she realised how very true it was. On the first night she had been so tired she had fallen asleep at once. On the second night, less sleepy, she had lain awake in the dark and listened to the extraordinary silence. She had become more accustomed than she had realised to the distant rhythm of traffic – not so much along the road where they had lived, but certainly along the main road that lay across its end. And in the old flat, when she first went to bed, there had often been the reassuring thump of Reggae from a flat or two along – not loud, nothing you had to listen to if you didn't want, just a sign that she was a part of the world and that normal lives were being lived all around her. Here, unless her mother made some sound downstairs, the only other lives she was aware of were the lives of birds, paddling with their clammy feet in a dark sea. And if her mother did make a tiny sound, its very tiny-ness made her more aware of their isolation.

The silence was like an emptiness that was waiting to be filled. She had realised that she was forcing herself to stay awake in order to hear what it was that would fill it. The longer the silence waited, and the sleepier she grew, the more overwhelming was the sense of something momentous about to happen.

At last she had begun to believe that two things were struggling for possession of her. One was sleep, which was creeping up on her like an incoming tide, and the other was some great change or revelation that was looming like a thunderstorm that can't quite break.

When she woke in the morning she knew that only one of the things had been real, sleep, and that it had won over the imaginary terror. But it had taken a while to win and as she frowned at the letter, which she could see wasn't going to be much fun for Sue to read, her eyes prickled with sleepiness.

"I'll tell you what there *is*," she wrote. "(It's shorter!) There's a man up here. He's bird-watching. He's great, you'd like him. He says I don't tell people things – so you'd agree with him right away. I went out with him yesterday and I want to go again today but Mum says I mustn't push it. Don't want to put him off, do I? I think I'll finish this now and post it. I'll feel better when I think you've got it. I'll feel we're still in the same world. Come to think of it, I haven't seen a pillar box, but I 'spose there must be one somewhere. Love, Lyn."

She addressed the envelope neatly and was just beginning to wonder what to do next when Bill turned up, with an invitation to look at the sparrow-like things. Despite the bulky anorak, he looked cold, and seemed so grateful to be offered coffee that Lyn could almost forgive him for the delay.

"You smell as if you've been out for hours," she said.

"Lyn!" said her mother spooning coffee from its jar in the kitchen.

"It's a nice smell," said Lyn defensively. It was too. It was a faint aura of salty mist which seemed to cling to the outsides of his clothes and to his hair, and which soon faded when enclosed in the small warm room. It smelt not so much like the sea itself as like a memory of the sea. She was hardly aware that it was the same smell she had found so thin and threatening when she had first encountered it.

"If you collect driftwood," said Bill, accepting his coffee and closing his hands tightly around the mug, "and burn it in that grate – it does work, you know – you get a very rich smell which is a bit similar. Though of course that's a warm smell and I imagine my anorak smells cold, doesn't it?"

Lyn nodded.

"I've been out since first light," said Bill. "It was very chilly then. It's not so bad now."

He had manoeuvred the upright chair in which he sat so that its back was against the wall, and now he stretched his legs out, right through the bars of the chair next to it, and leant one arm along the table top. It seemed to Lyn that he looked far too settled.

"We are going out in a minute, aren't we?" she said.

"We are."

"Give him a chance to rest, do," said her mother. Then she turned to Bill and spoke to him as though Lyn wasn't there at all. "She's been through her first evening – in I don't know how long – without television," she said, "and it's left her rather irritable and impatient, I'm afraid."

"I'm not," said Lyn, scowling.

"I'm not!" said her mother, imitating her, with an exaggerated downward turn to the corners of her mouth. At least, Lyn hoped it was exaggerated. She tried to keep her own expression just as it had been and wandered through into the bathroom to check on it.

"I didn't mean to offend you," her mother called after her. "Let's see that picture of the Estate."

Lyn examined her expression in the bathroom mirror. Not one of her better ones, she had to admit. She tried out a bright smile. But she let it fade when she realised she reminded herself of a particularly short-tempered dachshund she had once encountered on the Estate; it had fixed her with just such a wide stretched smile before lunging at her nearest ankle with an enthusiastic snarl. Fortunately, its lead had been just too short to allow its teeth to make contact with her. So she tried to form her features, instead, into a calm neutral sort of expression. But that only reminded her of the way people looked in the school photograph when they were hoping to be picked out as good examples. She gave up. "Over to you, face," she said quietly. "Do what you like."

"What? Can't hear you," called her mother.

"Nothing," said Lyn. She collected the Estate painting and brought it in to the table, lying it flat between the coffee mugs.

"Prop it up somewhere," said her mother. "It looks better."

"Can't," said Lyn, who couldn't be bothered.

Her mother stood up, then, and propped the picture neatly against the wall behind the table, securing it with the sugar bowl at one side and Lyn's empty milk glass at the other, each carefully placed so that they obscured as little of it as possible.

"Very imposing," said Bill. "Big, I should think."

"Mm," said Lyn.

"Why have you decided to make it float in the air? Is that to give it a sort of magical quality?"

"It doesn't float," said Lyn scornfully. "It's quite real."

"But it doesn't stand on the ground."

"You can't see the ground from where I was, that's all," said Lyn.

"If she snaps at you like that when you're out," said her mother to Bill, "send her home."

"Sorry, Lyn," said Bill unexpectedly, "didn't mean to pick on the painting. I was just interested. Shall we be off?"

Lyn was relieved to get out of the house – partly because she was beginning to find its small living room limiting, but mostly because she wanted Bill to herself. She didn't want to listen to him talking to someone else.

It looked quite different outside, with the mist all gone. It was like going into a different room, a larger one and of a different shape. The sea was visible right out to the place where it appeared to join the pale sky. There was even a faint grey line where the join seemed to be made, so that Lyn half-expected to see an arrowed label reading 'horizon'. Now that the immediate area was not shut in by the mist, like a scene in the glass bowl of a toy snowstorm, the horizon looked really promising, as though it led to other things, as though it would be perfectly possible to fly or sail beyond it and arrive, eventually, anywhere in the world one chose.

The views in each direction along the beach were opened up, too, and although there was obviously a limit to how far she could see, Lyn was, this time, aware that it was her eyes that were limited, not the world itself. The castle, way ahead, no longer looked like a structure built to mark the end of everything, it was just part of the view, and the beach and the low cliffs curved freely on beyond it.

There was altogether a tremendous sense of space, despite the fact that the tide was further in than it had been the previous day, making the beach narrower and, incidentally, bringing the birds at the water's edge conveniently closer.

The sun gave to the grey dune grass a touch of green and to the beige sand a touch of gold. The smell that Bill had brought in on his anorak was strong and rich outside – a mixture of salt and air and wetness, with a faintly bitter mineral undertow which was not at all unpleasant, and a slight though recognisable smell of grass. This was not the lush, luxurious smell of new-mown grass which makes you want to lie about in it, almost eat it. This was a sterner, more resilient yet fainter smell of living grass, working grass, grass which you had to respect because it would whip at your legs disapprovingly at any sign of sloppy behaviour, like rolling in it or snatching at handfuls of it. Nevertheless, you could play with it. Its flat coarse blades, pressed between the thumbs and blown through, produced the best owl noises and the best juggernaut-horn-imitations Lyn had ever heard.

The birds seemed to be out in force, although Bill still insisted this was nothing compared to how things would be in a month or so. There were Common Gulls and Black-Headed Gulls, though only one Herring Gull that they could see, and plenty of Great Black-Backed Gulls. The Diver was doing its act again, unless it was another one, and Bill said the Terns were beginning to arrive, although they were difficult to see because they were feeding rather far out. "There were a couple on the beach earlier on," he said. "We may get a better look another time."

As if to make up for the missing Terns, he showed her some Ringed Plovers, which he said had been there the day before as well. She realised she had vaguely noticed them, picking about around the flattish outcrop of rocks that joined the sea to the land, but she hadn't paid them much attention. Even through the binoculars they seemed quite small. They were beigey birds with white chests and important-looking black collars which they wore rather low, like very short bibs. They had a band of black across their foreheads and one just where their beaks joined their faces, and the two bands seemed to meet at the eye and then carry on past it and partly around the head, so that they looked a little as if they were wearing burglars' masks. They seemed intensely busy, running about on their thin yellow legs. Occasionally they stopped to bob their heads as if they felt their masks were slipping. Often they snatched at the sand, so rapidly that Lyn couldn't make out if they had picked anything up or not.

"Some of those little Burglar Bills have got messier patterns than others," said Lyn, adjusting the binoculars a little to see if that would improve their design. "Their masks have slipped down their fronts and they're not nearly as easy to see."

"Turnstones," said Bill. "All in amongst the Ringed Plovers. I wondered if you'd spot the difference. You're very good material, like it or not."

"Different birds, you mean?"

"Quite different. Very well camouflaged, wouldn't you say? Often you can't spot them at all, unless they fly off."

"Hang on," said Lyn. "Turnstones? Is that the same as Terns?"

"Oh no, entirely different. Tern is an old Norse word . . ."

"Hell-fire," said Lyn.

"Whereas – you'll like this bit – Turnstone is one of those nice easy names that simply describes the bird. It turns stones, looking for food, so it's a Turnstone. OK?"

"What beats me," said Lyn, "is what any of these birds eat, miles from anywhere like this."

"What can you mean?" said Bill. "They don't shop at Sainsbury's, you know."

"Back home," said Lyn, "they eat at MacDonald's."

"Don't tease me. I'm trying to educate you."

"It's true," said Lyn. "The pigeons hang around outside and eat chips and bits of bun. And when I've been to the seaside before, there've either been fishing boats and then the seagulls have followed them for bits of fish, or there've been fish and chips and things, and you can see them eating the leftovers."

"You know your trouble," said Bill, getting up slowly and brushing sand off himself. "You only look for what you hope to see, instead of looking at what's there. Come on, there's a good place along here where we can have a look inland."

"What do you mean?" said Lyn, following him up the sliding side of a dune.

"Well – you're fond of London and the Estate and all that that means, so when you get up here you insist on looking for it," said Bill stopping on the crest of the dune. "Naturally, you don't find it. So you decide this place is lacking. It isn't. Your Estate and your London pigeons and all that, they're still there, down south, living their lives. These birds are different, this is their estate, they're not dependent on people for food, they fish directly from the sea or dig up sandworms and tiny shellfish on the shore. I spotted it when I saw your painting."

"Oh, I know that's no good," said Lyn. "I'm not supposed to be an artist. Do you know, if you just bent your knees you'd look like a surfer on a sandwave?"

"The picture isn't bad at all," said Bill bending his corduroy knees and stretching his arms out. He raised his eyebrows at her.

"No good," said Lyn. "You look more like a suicide than a beach boy."

"But listen," said Bill, straightening up, unoffended. "You say you couldn't see the bottom of the Estate from where you were. That must mean there was something in the way?"

"The houses opposite," said Lyn, looking away from him. Her father would have done exactly that, pretended to be a surfer, though he'd probably have thought of it himself. Bill – who was not at all like her father, dark where he was fair, thickset where he was thin – suddenly looked wrong, badly made.

"Right!" said Bill. "But you weren't interested in them so you decided not to paint them. Well, that's your decision of course – but you mustn't mind if people think the Estate is floating in nothing."

In looking away from him, Lyn had turned towards the little house, even smaller with distance, and felt quite shocked to see the tiny figure of her mother outside it, wearing her bright red anorak and apparently looking towards them. Don't come and join us, Lyn willed her, don't, don't, don't. She was shaken to realise that, here, her mother could turn up any time she wanted to. The protection of that exclusive club called 'school' was gone.

"And it works the other way, too," Bill was saying. "Not only do you ignore what is there if it doesn't interest you – you put all your attention into looking for what you think does interest you, even if it obviously isn't there."

Go on, Lyn was thinking at her mother, go on, get in the car, go to the shops, you said it was expensive to hire it, get the most out of it, I'm OK, you can see I am, go on, drive off.

"When you look at this beach," said Bill, all unaware, "all you see is the lack of hot dog stands and postcard racks. No wonder it looks so bleak to you."

The small half-red figure turned and moved to the car, got in. The sound of the engine, unexpected in this place though so far away, made Bill turn to look.

"You're very unfair," said Lyn, elated by her success. "I've been looking at Plovers and Rolling Stones or whatever you call them for hours. I rather like them. I might even look at them again tomorrow."

The car reversed out of its scrubby parking place, paused, then drove slowly along the road past them, towards the village.

Keep going, thought Lyn, keep right on going. It did.

"Turnstones," said Bill automatically, waving as it went by. "Yes, I am being a bit heavy-handed. But you do take my point? I don't dispute that London pigeons eat chips.

But that doesn't mean that wild birds starve if there's no chippy around. I shouldn't think the birds here have ever eaten human-style food in their lives."

"Not even the Sandwich Turns?" said Lyn, grinning at him.

He laughed. "Not even them. They used to breed at a place called Sandwich in Kent. They don't now, but the name's stuck. Now shut up, and let's look for your little sparrow-like things in the buckthorn."

"Buckthorn is it?" said Lyn quietly, following him to the good vantage point. "It's going to wear my brain out if everything's going to turn out to have a name."

Behind them the sea hissed softly and sent wafts of its salty breath over their shoulders, and the birds called, and occasionally shrieked raucously, involved in some drama about the rightful ownership of a diminutive sand eel, but they faced resolutely away from all that, watching the scrubby buckthorn bushes and the flat hinterland for signs of movement.

Bill showed her how to keep the binoculars well clear of the damaging grains of sand – and how to use her detached anorak hood as a leaning pad if she had to lower them near its surface. He also produced, from one of the amazingly capacious pockets of his own anorak, a camera with an extendable lens. He explained its workings to her in some detail, and then showed her how to use it as a substitute for the binoculars, without actually taking a picture. "If I'm using either of them," he said, "and you want to see something, help yourself to the other one, you don't need to ask."

"Thanks," said Lyn.

The camera lens was not quite so powerful as the extra-ordinary binoculars, but it was still extremely effective, and Lyn rather fancied herself looking through it. The binoculars were so small that an ignorant passer-by could have mistaken them for a toy, while the camera was quite obviously the real thing. Not that there were any passers-by, ignorant or otherwise; apart from Mr Parker and the dog, who didn't in any case pass by but remained tiny in the distance, plodding steadily along near the foot of the castle cliffs.

This bit of beach was between two bird sanctuaries, Bill said, one further up the coast, one a little bit south and inland, and most of the bird watchers went to one or the other. Also, this was a fairly quiet time of year. Autumn, winter and, soon, the breeding season were worst, he said. At busy times you might not be able to see a Snow Bunting for the clusters of bird-watchers grouped around its chosen bush.

"Must be a bit like being a pop star," said Lyn.

They did see Snow Buntings, though, one first, then a flock of four, little brownish sparrow-looking things to Lyn's eye, until they spread their almost wholly white wings and flew, dipping and lifting away across the ground.

"Aren't they great when they fly?" said Lyn, amazed. "It's like Cinderella putting on her ball gown."

"Are they the ones you saw before?"

"Might have been," said Lyn. "I didn't pay much attention before. But I think I'd have noticed the white."

"They'll be gone soon."

"Where?"

"Up north. To breed."

"Everything's on the move."

"Oh yes. Very few of the birds that've wintered here will breed here. And the ones who do breed here are just beginning to arrive, in ones and twos."

"Like the Turns?"

"Like the Terns."

He also pointed out a Skylark, a group of Fieldfares – a Blackbird which Lyn had recognised on her own but hadn't liked to mention in case she was wrong – a Redwing which she had thought was a female Blackbird – a Greenfinch – and a Yellow-hammer, which refused to say 'A little bit of bread and no cheese' as all the school books said it did.

"It'll say it in summer," said Bill. "At least, it'll be quite vocal. What you think it's saying is another matter. It's never sounded like anything to do with bread and cheese to me."

Suddenly, he looked at his watch. "What time do you usually have lunch?" he said.

"Oh – twelve-thirty or one, I suppose."

"You and me both," said Bill. "We'll be shot. Come on."

Lyn expected they would only walk together as far as the Parkers' house and that she would then go on on her own, but he accompanied her beyond the Parkers' without her even noticing because, as they progressed along the road, she suddenly realised that she couldn't see the hired car parked in the usual place. Even though the road was not straight so that she wouldn't have expected to see the whole car, she felt sure she should see at least its back half. But she couldn't. It was lunchtime – it was after lunchtime – her mother had never, in all her memory, failed to be at home with food ready at the appointed time. Therefore if she was not back there must be a good reason for it – or more likely a bad one. A crash. She had never been much of a one for driving, Lyn remembered, and since her father and the car had left home she had had months off the road – and this car was hired, and new to her.

"We could all go beachcombing this afternoon, for wood," said Bill. "If you like. I haven't really bothered since the last onshore winds and there's plenty lying around."

I should have let her come with us this morning, Lyn thought, not sent her off in that car, why did I do that, what can have happened?

"OK?" said Bill.

"OK," said Lyn with feeling. Only a few more steps they'd taken, but there it was, the back end of the car, and then, as they continued, the rest of it. She'd tucked it further in beside the house, that was all. Seeing it there, Lyn remembered that she hadn't made her mother go away at all, it had all been in her head.

"I didn't hear the car come back," she said.

"I saw her drive past when you were watching the Snow Buntings," said Bill. "But I told you before – you don't hear much down in the dunes."

Lyn's mother took their lateness quite calmly and looked pleased by Lyn's quick hug. She seemed to like the idea of beachcombing for firewood.

"It would save using the electric one," she said. "And it is still quite cold in the evenings."

"We'll take Mr Parker's pushchair," said Bill, "and get plenty for both houses."

"Mr Parker's *pushchair*?" said Lyn.

"He got it when Buster twisted his leg – so you can imagine it's quite big. He used to push him out as far as the castle and then they'd both walk home – with Buster getting in every now and then for a bit more of a ride." He raised his eyebrows at Lyn. "As long as you're not ashamed to be seen with me," he said, "shoving a pushchair along like an old tramp."

"Oh, I can handle it," said Lyn. "If nothing else it'll be something to put in a letter to Sue."

Chapter Eleven

More of the smaller, yellow and black beaked birds were arriving.
They joined those that were already there and they, too, seemed to
accept the larger, red-beaked bird. They began to show more
interest in the shore. Later they would colonise a stretch of beach,
and scratch out dips in the sand in which to lay their eggs. It wasn't
time yet, the bulk of the breeding colony had not even arrived.
Nevertheless, these early arrivals were drawn to land for spells of
time – though they still retired out to sea to feed.

In the end they all went beachcombing. Mrs Parker put on
what she called her 'rough mac', an old gaberdine of Mr
Parker's that reached down almost to her ankles and so
protected her jumper and skirt from the odd-shaped bits of
wood they had picked up, some of which had nails stuck in
them, or oily patches in hidden places. She pushed the
pushchair slowly along the road, gripping its handle with
apparently empty sleeves since she didn't bother to turn
back the overlong cuffs, keeping pace with the others who
were scavenging on the beach-side of the dunes. At regular
intervals, Lyn carried their haul across the sandy barrier
and stashed it on the seat. As the load grew, Mrs Parker
took to strapping it in, like a huge, many-legged baby, a
wooden octopus.

Mr Parker didn't bother to collect anything, he just
sought out smooth light sticks which he threw for Buster.
He didn't throw them very far, and Buster certainly never
ran, but rocked his way across to each stick, picked it up as
though it was the most awkward shape imaginable, and
then rocked slowly back with it. "Memories of better times,"

said Mr Parker, as he bent carefully to accept the first returned stick and to praise Buster for his efforts.

Bill walked along the very edge of the dunes, just where they joined the flat sand, scuffing his feet and uncovering bleached driftwood which he gathered; plastic bottles and paper cups and broken bits and pieces which he ignored or covered up again; and occasionally a shell or a shiny piece of sea coal which he passed to Lyn.

Lyn followed him, sometimes helping to pick up driftwood, but mostly carrying it to the patiently pacing Mrs Parker.

Lyn was aware of her mother following behind her, strolling along with her hands behind her back, her hair being blown by the chilly breeze. She didn't pick anything up, but seemed quite happy, looking out to sea with the kind of stretched smile people wear when the sky is too bright but they don't mind it. When Lyn passed the shells on to her she looked at them with the same smile, didn't comment but, when requested, put them carefully in the pocket of her anorak, sometimes wrapping a particularly delicate one in a paper hanky so that it shouldn't be crushed against the others.

"I've been thinking," said Lyn to Bill, during one of the times she was keeping pace with him, waiting to take on board the next assignment of pale wood, "when we go – will I ever see you again?"

"I should think so. I only live about forty or so miles from your new place. And you may even come up to this horrible beach on holiday again, who knows." He piled her arms with wood. "Off you go, quickly, before you drop it all."

"I'll stay this side till we're level with that break," said Lyn, trying to point with her eyes, since her hands were occupied, at a gap between two dunes that seemed to hairpin back on itself and run parallel to them. "You can't see from here, but there's a quick way through to the road just round the corner in there."

"Neatly spotted," said Bill. Then, as she disappeared into the sandy ravine of her short cut, he called after her, "See how the pushchair looks, with that load in it. I should think it's about full."

"It is full," said Lyn when she returned. "Mrs Parker's taking it home. She says if we'll all follow she'll have the kettle on."

Instead, Bill just stopped kicking at the drifted sand for buried firewood and sat down, looking out to sea. So Lyn sat down beside him. Her mother wandered slowly towards them from one direction and Mr Parker and Buster were closing in from the other.

"Everybody's run out of puff," said Lyn

Mr Parker and Buster sat themselves heavily down on the far side of Bill. Lyn's mother sat down beside her – after a brief pause during which she looked as though she might be going to say something about dampness, or sand in the clothes. However, if she had been going to, she changed her mind without a word.

"We must look as if we're waiting for the show to begin," said Lyn. "All sitting in a row like this."

Bill laughed.

"We may wait forever," said Mr Parker gloomily, from beyond him.

"Don't worry about it," said Bill easily.

"Well," said Mr Parker. "Well, well, well." He rubbed the dog's head vigorously, so that its whole heavy body rocked from side to side. "Bringing you all the way up here."

"No problem," said Bill. "I'm having a nice time."

Lyn was embarrassed. If they must talk about their secret in front of her, she wished they'd at least lower their voices. "Shall I show you some Turnstones?" she said to her mother.

"Yes, all right." Lyn was secretly pleased to see that her mother was preparing to rise obligingly to her feet. She expected to be led to the Turnstones. She probably thought they were rocks or pebbles of some kind, Lyn realised. She put out a hand to restrain her. "They're birds," she said kindly. "They're usually over near those rocks. I'll just make sure."

Bill had the miniature binoculars up to his eyes and was scanning the beach slowly and steadily, rather as the grey-haired ornithologist had the day before. Mr Parker, equipped with a more normal-sized pair, was doing the same thing. They looked, Lyn thought, like a pair of overgrown owls. She reached into Bill's nearside anorak pocket and found the camera. Without lowering the glasses or pausing in his systematic survey, Bill swayed very slightly towards her so that the pocket fell further open and she could withdraw the camera easily. She looped the strap around her neck, took off the lens cap and slipped it back into his pocket, and raised the camera to her eyes. She was pleased to see that she was getting better at pointing the thing in the right direction. She found the rocks at once, and a blur of birds. Holding the camera as steadily as she could with her left hand, she extended the long lens with her right, pulling it out with her hand underneath it for support, as Bill had shown her. But just as she had got the focal length right, and just as she was confirming for herself that the Turnstones were busy among the fussy little Ringed Plovers, her mother's voice made her jump.

"Lyn! What are you doing? You mustn't use that, you'll break it."

Lyn lowered the camera from her eyes to find that her mother was trying, very gently, to take it away from her – difficult since the strap was still safely around her neck.

But before she could protest, Bill leant across her, "No, no, that's fine," he said. "Lyn knows how to use it."

"But she mustn't take photos with such an expensive camera," said her mother, looking at him in wide-eyed amazement, and still cradling the Pentax in her hands, as if afraid to let it go.

"She's just using it as substitute binoculars," said Bill, "while these are occupied. Found the Turnstones, Lyn?"

"Well, I *had* . . ." Lyn began indignantly, "before . . ."

"Show your mother how to get them in the camera sights, then," said Bill easily, interrupting her. "Unless she knows already, of course."

"Believe it or not, I've never used one," said Lyn's mother. "Not even to take photographs." She looked at Lyn and smiled. "I'm sorry," she said. "I didn't realise. Now, how do we move so that we don't both let go at once and drop it between us?"

"You let go," said Lyn loftily, "and I'll pass it to you when you're ready." She would have rather liked to press home her advantage, somehow draw attention all over again to the fact that she had been in the right and her mother in the wrong, but couldn't see how, when her mother had already apologised. Then it occurred to her that it might be as boring for everyone else if she went on and on about it as it was boring for her when her mother went on and on about things. So she gave up and tried to pass on the little she had picked up about the birds.

"Ah well," said Mr Parker at last. "We'd better be getting back – didn't I hear you say May was putting the kettle on?"

"Yes," said Lyn, relieved. She was quite ready to move now everyone was staring through some kind of lens except for her.

"Is she expecting us?" said her mother, lowering the camera at once.

"She is," said Mr Parker, struggling a little where he sat but not actually rising. Bill got to his feet and pulled him up.

"Well, we must go." She hesitated for a moment with the camera, and looked across at Bill. Bill smiled at her, but didn't hold out his hand. She returned the smile, nodded, and handed the camera to Lyn. Lyn retrieved the lens cap from Bill's pocket, replaced it, and then stashed the camera away. Her mother, Mr Parker and Buster were already setting off across the dunes.

"I wish I had been taking a photo," said Lyn wistfully. "Of all of us. For a reminder."

"You can take one now if you want to," said Bill.

"No, thanks. It's too late now we're on the move. It would have to have been of all of us, with Mrs Parker and her mac and her pushchair."

"She'd never have allowed that!" Mr Parker called back over his shoulder. "Only a few privileged people are allowed to see her looking like that."

"Paint a picture," said Bill.

"No one would believe it."

"They might. It'd be a bit like a Lowry."

"What's that?"

"He was someone who might have painted us. Here, take a last look through the binocs. There are the famous Terns I've been telling you about – there are four or five today, down on the beach by the breakwater."

Under his guidance Lyn found them, white like seagulls but more streamlined, with black legs too short for their bodies and long tail feathers that stuck out behind.

"A bit like seagulls," she said cautiously.

"Their tails are very deeply forked – you can see it when they fly – and they have narrower heads and finer beaks."

"And untidy hair," said Lyn. "In fact they look as if they're wearing little wigs."

"Wigs!" said Bill. "It's known as a crest in the best circles." But it was true that the dark feathers on their rather flat heads stuck straight out at the back instead of lying smoothly and all-of-a-piece down their necks. "Now, those rather patchily dark heads . . ." he went on.

"Don't tell me," said Lyn. "They turn purple and green in summer."

"Only black I'm afraid. And if you really want to get into

this identification thing, try to see if you can get a good look at their beaks. The Sandwich Terns are the only European ones to have black beaks with yellow tips."

"What!" said Lyn, lowering the glasses, the effort of concentrating making her feel she was going cross-eyed. "You mean there are other sorts of Terns?"

"Oh yes, not half."

"That come here?"

"Sometimes. Now let's follow the others back for tea. I happen to know Mrs Parker is going to make a fire with their share of the wood, and we're all going to toast crumpets."

"Not sandwiches?"

"Not sandwiches! Still, pretty civilised, eh?"

"Not half," said Lyn.

The tea party was fun. They all sat around the fire, watching each other's faces grow blotches in the heat and telling each other off for putting too much butter on the crumpets. Later, when all hands had been wiped or washed free of grease, Mr Parker got out his notebooks and showed off the records he'd kept over the years.

"Don't bore them," said Mrs Parker, trying to protect Lyn and her mother from his enthusiasm. But, a little to her own surprise, Lyn found she was actually interested. Mr Parker explained that a true birdwatcher didn't just learn to recognise birds, but noted down numbers, dates – and often even wind direction which might explain why some migrating birds were early or late, hurried on or held back by following or head winds.

"Or even blown off course altogether," he said, closing the last book. "It's always an extra little perk to see something rare, or something hundreds of miles from where it should be."

"Like the Sandpiper in Wales?" said Lyn to Bill.

"Yes, like that," said Mr Parker, who clearly knew all the same stories. "Though it's wise to remember that if you think you've glimpsed something extraordinarily rare, you're almost certainly mistaken.''

After that Mrs Parker got out a double pack of cards and the five of them played Racing Demon. The game built up such an outrageous speed that even Lyn's mother was driven to let out demonic shrieks of success or failure.

And eventually, when they were ready to leave and Bill said he would help carry their share of the wood home through the early beginnings of dusk, Mr Parker looked out a pair of binoculars, the old-fashioned rather heavy kind that Lyn recognised, and told her that she could have them. At first her mother protested, but he only smiled, and apologised for their weight. "You'll need a lighter, more powerful pair one of these days," he said. "Put them on your Christmas list, maybe."

"Oh no, I like these," said Lyn, holding their important weight in her hands and sniffing at the interesting smell of their leather bindings. She had a feeling that these binoculars, being old and much used, would have a better idea of where to look than new ones would. She felt she was still too new herself to run in new equipment successfully. "I like these very much. Thank you."

Chapter Twelve

Bill was not always available. He was out among the dunes for long spells of time, perhaps on his own, perhaps with Mr Parker. Knowing that he could not escape from her if she chose to track him down, and not wanting to risk being sent packing, Lyn let him be. Sometimes she watched on her own, through her new-old binoculars, from the dunes directly opposite the house, knowing that his favourite hides were farther along, on the way to the castle. On these occasions she did her best to make her own identifications with the help of a very small bird book she had found behind a packet of custard powder in the village shop. She noted down her sightings in a small account book, with irritating vertical lines down its pages, which was the only notebook this same Post Office shop had been able to offer.

Sometimes she went in to the village with her mother, who made the trip at least once a day, even though there was so little there. It was a one-street village and usually, when they drove in, theirs was the only vehicle moving – though once they had seen the Royal Mail Van. The Post Office and General Stores was really the main shop, and it even had a tiny deep-freeze full of fish fingers and peas and Arctic Rolls, as well as three shelves of baked beans and tea bags and floor polish. There was also a bakery, that smelt particularly good in the mornings and did a nice line in individual cakes with bright pink icing that Lyn found very appealing. There was a dairy, that delivered to all the outlying houses as well as to the village itself, and you could go in to the Accounts Office, that led on to the cool store, and buy butter and yoghourt and cartons of milk.

There was a butcher that opened in the afternoons only, a

church that shared its vicar with two others and was locked except for Sunday mornings and Tuesday late afternoons when two or three, including the vicar, attended Evensong.

And there was a pub, with an interesting picture on its sign, called the Crow and Anchor, which the butcher said had once been the Crown and Anchor. The N had dropped off so many years ago, he said, that when a new sign was needed the landlord had forgotten to tell the signpainter about it, which was why he had painted a large black bird perched on one of the points of a beached anchor.

"A bit like the Y in Barney," Lyn had said, mainly to herself, and then had discovered that the butcher had plenty of time to lean on his counter and question her until he had got the whole story, plus a description of the Estate, and of several of the people who lived in it. He had soon got on to the subject of what she and her mother might be doing in these parts and Lyn, who was in any case rather sick of the smell of blood and sawdust, had been relieved when her mother had said rapidly that they were on a bird-watching holiday and had manoeuvred them both out of the door.

"A white lie," she had said, somehow apologetically, when they were outside.

"Not a lie at all," said Lyn. "I am bird-watching." That was when they had bought the book and notebook at the Post Office.

Sometimes she tried to paint the sea, sighing a lot as she did so, not so much because it wouldn't keep still, which was only to be expected, as because it would keep changing colour, which seemed less reasonable.

But a couple of times a day at least Bill did fetch her, to take her off on a tiny expedition to show her things he had spotted.

Once it was to watch a Cormorant, standing on one of the uprights of the breakwater, holding out its wings to dry them. Its dark distinctive shape and its stillness turned the breakwater post into a Roman Standard. "I expect to see Roman Legionnaires marching down to pick it up and carry it in to battle," said Lyn. "Do you?" said Bill. "No, I think I expect to see it joined by a Pterodactyl. It's got such a primitive sort of reptilian head, don't you think?"

Once it was in the hope of showing her a single Hooded Crow, inland, and just passing through, but by the time they had reached the right spot it had gone. "Passed right through," said Lyn resignedly, and explained about the Crow and Anchor, which Bill said he had visited but never questioned.

Although they quite often had tea or coffee all together, sometimes with the Parkers and sometimes not, Lyn's mother didn't join them again on any of their expeditions. Lyn was glad of this, and told Bill so.

"Why?" he said.

She didn't really know, although she thought it probably had something to do with the fact that she felt older when she had Bill to herself. "You don't talk to me like I'm a child," she said at last. "She does."

"You have to bring parents up properly, you know," said Bill unexpectedly.

"What do you mean?"

"Well – all this training – it's not a one-way thing. Mr Parker may have trained Buster to fetch the sticks he throws, but over the years Buster has trained Mr Parker to throw smooth sticks, that are comfortable on the mouth."

"What should I train my mother to do?" said Lyn. She picked up a long grey wing feather from the sand and threw it like a dart. She threw so that the light wind followed it and it went a surprisingly long way. "Fetch?" she said.

Bill laughed. "You have to train her to know you're growing up, that you can understand more, do more, than she realises."

"That's obvious."

"It isn't. You drop about three years when you're with her, did you know that?"

"It's because of the way she treats me. She treats me too young."

"It isn't her fault. She's known you since you were a helpless tadpole. You can't expect her to guess you're capable of more unless you show her."

Lyn fetched the feather and stroked its stiff soft barbs across her cheek. "How?" she said, finding that she wasn't entirely pleased to be discussing her mother at all.

"You know how," said Bill. "Think about it."

"I don't."

"As soon as you showed her you knew how to handle the camera, she accepted that you could. She handed it back to you when she'd finished with it, not to me."

"Only because you tipped her the wink. I saw you."

"Well, what about when you offered to show her the Turnstones? She was pleased. She looked where you pointed, she listened while you told her what they eat. You tell her things, she'll tell you things. She's basically all right, your mother, but she 'could do better'. It's up to you. Hey! Did you see that!"

"It was one of your Turns," said Lyn, as the bird circled over them and headed out to sea again. Bill trained his glasses on its disappearing figure and then shook his head. "Didn't get a good look," he said.

"But you know a Turn when you see one," said Lyn. "Even I do."

"Hm," he lowered the glasses. "Well don't let it Tern your head."

"I do like going out with you," said Lyn. "How stupid that I ran away that first time. I missed a whole morning of you."

Bill let go of the glasses so that they hung from their strap. He took her by the shoulders and turned her to face him. "Never, never think that," he said. His face was very serious.

"What do you mean?" said Lyn, startled.

"Think! It could have been anyone. There are some funny people about. No, Lyn, don't laugh, I mean this."

"You mean 'don't take binoculars from a stranger'?"

"I do mean that."

"Well I didn't, did I?" said Lyn, wriggling free, flustered. "I ran."

"I know. And you were right, because even though it was only me, being stupid and not realising I shouldn't follow you, it might not have been. It can be a nasty world – you do have to check people out."

"Look," said Lyn, walking away from him, "I know that, don't I? You're sounding like her now. How is it that I do the right thing, and then I get into trouble because I *might* not have done it? That's not fair."

He came up beside her and they walked slowly along the dune tops together. "You're right," he said. "I'm not being fair. I'm sorry. It was just what you said, that's all."

Lyn made no comment.

"Sit down a minute," said Bill. "I want to show you a picture."

They sat in a dip, their backs sheltered by a wall of grassy sand, and Bill produced from one of his enormous inside pockets quite a small bird book.

"Birds of North America?" said Lyn, as he opened it. "Of *North America*?"

He passed it to her, tapping one of the pictures with his finger, a picture of a white bird, with a flat crested head and a deeply forked tail.

"One of your Turns," said Lyn.

"Look again."

"It's got a red beak – not black with yellow." She looked at the top of the page. "A Royal Tern," she said. "Oh – Tern. Why didn't you tell me it was spelt like that? I've been saying Turn."

For a moment she stared at him quite indignantly, and

then began to laugh with him as she realised. "Well, what about it?" she said, then.

"That – there – is our secret, Mr Parker's and mine. He thought he saw a Royal Tern, about a week ago, far out to sea with two or three of the Sandwich Terns. It shouldn't be here, it should be in North America. It's possible, just possible, that one got blown off course and ended up here, though it's extremely unlikely. But if it did – it would be only the third or fourth sighting in this country ever. He was so excited he rang me, and I changed all my plans and came up. Since then he hasn't seen it again, and I haven't seen it at all, and now he's panicking, thinking he was mistaken."

"And is it here?"

"We don't know. It's what we're looking for. It's why I didn't want our migratory ornithologist to twig there might be something special here."

"You want to see it – and not her to see it?"

"Partly. It's mainly that if you're not wild about someone you don't want them hanging around. And if she thought she might see a Royal Tern, she'd glue herself to the beach for as long as it took."

"Was it this that you thought flew over us this morning?"

"I wondered. But I didn't get a good look. It may all be a false alarm – it doesn't matter, it was worth the trip just on the offchance. But just in case it wasn't a false alarm – and I'd be surprised if Mr Parker made a mistake – you mustn't tell a soul. You'd be amazed how word can travel."

"And we'd have eight million ornithologists crawling all over this beach?" said Lyn.

He regarded her solemnly. "Possibly just short of eight million," he said. "But more than would be comfortable."

"If you see it," said Lyn, "do they name it after you or something."

"No, but you 'go down in the annals'. It's quite a performance, actually. We'd tell the Bird Recorder for this county, and then we'd have to fill in a form for the County

Records Committee, and if they were convinced they'd pass the news to the National Records Committee, and eventually the sighting would be published in '*British Birds*', with the name of whoever spotted it."

"And sucks boo to your lady ornithologist?"

"Certainly not! I'm a mature and reasonable bird-watcher – I would simply follow the correct procedure for registering a rare bird, that's all. No, truly, it would just be very exciting to see it. If I confirm the sighting we'd send it in under Mr Parker's name, anyway."

"And I don't even tell my mum?"

"You don't tell anyone. If each person tells just one person they trust, it isn't long before everyone knows."

"Should you have told me?"

"If I didn't, you wouldn't know it was special if you spotted it."

"You think *I* might see it?"

"Anyone might."

"Let's go and watch the Sandwich Terns now, then."

They watched until Lyn's tea-time, but the Terns were far out to sea, and even the astonishingly powerful miniature binoculars didn't reveal anything out of the ordinary.

"You'd better get back," said Bill. "It's nearly dusk. I'll tell you if I see anything. Or if Mr Parker does."

Lyn ran back to the little house, sometimes skipping sideways as she went. I've got a secret, she thought, in time to her steps. I know something special. I might find it – it might be me, it might be me.

"You're looking very perky," said her mother, as Lyn hurried in through the unlocked front door. "Is it because you're looking forward to tomorrow?"

"What's tomorrow?" said Lyn.

"I *did* tell you – when the letter came. I remember telling you the moment I read it. We're going up to Gran and Grandpop's for the day."

Lyn sat down on the fireside chair opposite her. The side

light by her mother's chair was on, and she and her book and part of the mantelpiece and rug glowed warmly in the dim room. Lyn reached out and put on her own light, and saw how it enlivened the colour of her jeans and sneakers and even her hands in her lap. It had grown dark indoors much earlier than out and the two small bright pools of light made the rest of the room look even dimmer than when only one had been lit.

"Yes, I remember now," said Lyn. She looked at the neat pile of broken-up driftwood in the grate.

"Now you *don't* look so perky. You want to see them, don't you?"

"Course I do. I just didn't realise we were going so soon."

"Only for the day."

"I know. Can I light the fire?"

Her mother considered for a moment, then made a slight face at her. "I don't really like to think of you playing with fire," she said.

"I'd be careful. I am quite sensible."

Her mother smiled. "I know," she said apologetically. "But I think I'd better do it this time – I'm not even very sure of it myself yet. The chimney blows it back at you a bit sometimes."

"Will there be time to go on the beach first, tomorrow?"

"I'd rather you didn't. I'd like to get going because I'd like to get back before dark. Why?"

"Oh – I just wanted to look for a bird."

"You've been looking at birds for days."

"There are birds and birds," said Lyn. She slid down on to her knees in front of the grate and clapped her hands. "Come on," she said, "jump to it. I want to watch you light it so I can learn how."

Her mother put down her book, reached up for the matchbox on the corner of the mantelpiece and knelt down beside her. "I can't," she said, beginning to laugh. "It'll put me off, you watching."

"You may find I give advice," said Lyn. "But don't worry about it, you don't have to take it."

"Well all right. But don't blame me if I can't get it to draw at once."

"That won't matter," said Lyn. "I'm very tolerant."

The first match caught the few balls of screwed up newspaper at the very bottom of the small construction of wood, and blossomed into a little flame that tiptoed delicately among the bleached strips of bark and the central bird's nest of sticks. When it was in command of all those it flirted with the two tiny logs, and at last got a firm foothold on them, too. That was when it began to make a confident crackling noise.

"Very good," said Lyn. "I could have done that. I'll do it tomorrow."

Her mother gave her a quick hug. "We'll see," she said, and went out in to the kitchen to think about tea.

Chapter Thirteen

Lyn stood in her grandparents' small sitting room regarding the stuffed parrot, which was firmly wired to its perch. It had been a Macaw, coloured in vivid blue and red, and although its colours were a bit faded now she could still just remember it when it had been alive. As a very small child she had been fascinated by it and a little afraid of it. Although it had never pecked her – or anyone else – its beak looked hard and fierce and there was something witch-like about the pale wrinkled feet which used to clasp and unclasp around the perch as they shuffled drily along it and back again. It had never talked, but sometimes it had raised its harsh voice in a triumphant-sounding shriek that had never failed to make her jump. It had always spent a lot of time sitting on her grandmother's shoulder, usually leaning forward to watch intently whatever she was doing. In particular it had watched Lyn, out of one eye and then out of the other, staring and staring, somehow looking wise and rather amused at the same time. Bird-watching, Lyn thought now, touching its cold silky head very gently.

When it had died there had been great discussions about what to do with it – they had none of them then known anyone with a garden who would be able to bury it for them. Lyn couldn't remember exactly what had happened, probably she had never known, but she was fairly sure that it was her grandfather who had arranged for this to be done to it, as a surprise for her grandmother. The surprise, it seemed, had been a pleasant one, and now here it sat, quite still, in the corner of the room, its head slightly on one side, still watching, through one glass eye.

Lyn had never been able to decide what she thought of it,

now that it was dead. Part of her found it rather disgusting, especially when her grandmother flicked over it with a feather duster. Part of her found it rather classy – after all, no one else's grandmother had a stuffed parrot. Today she realised she was in three minds about it, instead of the usual two. The third part found it weird the way circumstances could force you to watch a dead and familiar parrot, when what you really wanted to watch for was a live and rare Tern.

"I wish you could have stayed here," her grandmother was saying. "If only we had a second bedroom."

"We're fine where we are," said her mother. "It's very cosy, isn't it Lyn?"

Lyn went over and sat on the sofa by her grandmother, who automatically put an arm around her. "It's great in the evenings," she said, "when the fire gets going."

"What do you mean?" said her grandfather. "Gets going?"

"Well, I mean sometimes it goes out at first, and Mum has to start it again," said Lyn, lounging comfortably against her grandmother. "It was really good last night, though. I think we're getting the hang of it."

"You mean an open fire?" said her grandfather. "A live fire?" He was sitting forward in his chair with his hands on the ends of the arms. When he did this it meant either that he was about to get up or else that he was about to disapprove strongly about something. He didn't get up.

"We burn driftwood," said her mother.

"I don't like the sound of that," said her grandfather, his fingertips pressing in to the chair arms.

"It sounds good," said Lyn, and giggled. "It crackles."

"Now Lyn," said her grandmother, giving her a quick hug with the encircling arm. "Your grandfather's worried."

"It's very economical," said her mother. "In fact, it's free."

"No," said her grandfather. "No, I don't think it's a good

idea. I don't like the thought of the two of you playing with fire.''

"We're not *playing* with it," said her mother, her voice pitched slightly higher than usual so that it sounded rather plaintive. "We're using it to keep warm in the evenings."

"Haven't you any other form of heating?"

"An electric fire – but that costs money – and I am trying to be careful with money."

"No one who runs a car is being careful with money," said her grandfather. He had been cheery over lunch, telling them about the party at work the week before, thrown in honour of his retirement. But the cheer had gone now.

"It's only a hired car," said her mother, and, "She needs a car, Dad," said her grandmother, more or less at once.

"You should have hired it for the day to drive your stuff up, then given it back and hired it for another day when you move in up here."

"Oh Dad, then they couldn't have come up here today."

"There is public transport – there are buses – I've got through sixty years now without a car. This generation expects things too easy."

"I need it," said her mother, "to get to the shops. It's two miles to the village, you know. It's not like here or London where you step out of the door and there are food shops in every direction. I take it you don't want us to starve down there. Or perhaps you do. That would be a big saving, wouldn't it, if I stopped buying food?"

"Don't be childish, lovey," said her grandmother.

"Well, he's so unreasonable."

"Let's forget the car," said her grandfather, "you've already had it so long I don't suppose a few days'll make much difference. But you're to stop these open fires. You're not used to them – and I won't have your mother lying awake at night picturing you both incinerated down there."

Her mother got up and walked quickly across the room.

"I'll make some tea," she said, without looking at anyone. She went out of the room and shut the door firmly behind her.

Her grandfather let go of the arms of the chair and sat back a bit further. "Try and talk sense to her and she just goes slamming out of the room," he said, half to himself.

"Oh no, she didn't slam it," said her grandmother. "I don't think you need worry so much, Dad, she's a sensible girl really."

Lyn wriggled out of her grandmother's embrace. "I'll go and help get tea," she said.

"You know what?" said Lyn to her mother in the kitchen.

"What," said her mother flatly, without looking round. She was spooning tea into a blue and white teapot.

"You haven't brought them up properly."

"What *do* you mean?" She was so surprised that she actually turned her back on the teapot and looked at Lyn.

"Well you haven't trained them to know that you're grown-up."

Her mother stared at her for a moment, and then began to laugh. It was only when her face relaxed into its laugh that Lyn realised how pinched it had been just before. "However am I to do that?" she said.

"I'm not sure. I think you have to impress them with your abilities."

The kettle began to whistle. "Quick," said her mother, picking it off the gas and filling the teapot. "Finish laying the tray."

"We'll go on having the fire, won't we?" said Lyn, adding teaspoons to the saucers. "We're quite safe with it."

"Yes, we will, but don't mention it again, they'll let it drop if they're not reminded about it."

"I'm sorry I said about it."

"Oh that's all right," said her mother. "You couldn't know. I'd have mentioned it myself if you hadn't. I always forget how he worries."

"He said Grandma would worry."

"No, it's him. He can't admit it, but it's him. He went through a very big war, when he was very young, and it made him too aware of dangers. When I was your age I wasn't even allowed to go to school on my own. Did you know that?" She picked up the tray.

"No," said Lyn, opening the door for her. "No, you never told me before."

"Thank you," said her grandmother, receiving the tray on to the side table by the sofa, "that's very kind."

"We ought to be off in about an hour. I don't want to get back too late."

"That's all right, lovey. Oh, I so wish we could have managed that surprise for you."

"Not to worry."

"What surprise?" said Lyn.

"We were going to show you your new home – it was all fixed – that's why we asked you for today and not at the weekend. But at the last minute the silly people have gone off to see about the house they want – it's very annoying."

"They've gone to exchange contracts," said Lyn's grandfather, accepting a cup of tea and sitting well back in his chair. "They hope. If all goes well they'll have a moving date by the time they get back. That's not annoying – it's what we've all been waiting for."

"I'd like Lyn to have seen it, though," said her grandmother.

"Oh, no," said Lyn suddenly flustered, "I wouldn't want to – not with other people in it – other people's things – "

"You'll be glad when it's settled though, won't you. Are you very bored down in that funny little house?"

"No, it's OK," said Lyn, but even as she answered her grandmother was turning to her mother. "Is she still having those educational walks with that friend of the Moores?" she said.

"Bill. Yes."

Educational, thought Lyn, that was a death-dealing word.

"We never met him, did we?"

"No," said her mother. "I'd never met him either. It was only when we were talking, with him and Mr Parker, that I remembered the Moores mentioning him. I think they see quite a lot of him – and he uses the house twice a year, regularly."

"Well, come on then," said her grandmother. "We haven't heard any details. What's he like? Lyn, you tell me."

"Oh," said Lyn. "Well – I don't know."

"He's nice, is he?"

"I wouldn't go for walks with him if he wasn't."

"Lyn," said her mother warningly.

"And is he married?"

"I don't know," said Lyn. It hadn't occurred to her to wonder. He seemed so complete, out there on the beach, she hadn't tried to picture him in any other situation. An odd thought struck her, and it gave her a peculiar feeling she didn't understand. "I never even asked him if he had any children," she said.

"He isn't," said her mother, finishing her tea and putting her cup back on the tray. "And he hasn't."

"So he hasn't got a little girl your age, Lyn," said her grandmother. "Perhaps that's why he likes you so much."

Lyn scowled down into her empty cup. She hadn't wondered about Bill liking her, either, had just accepted his friendship. Somehow, she didn't enjoy the idea of his seeing her as a substitute daughter. "It isn't that," she said with sulky conviction. "It's that we've got interests in common."

"Interests in common!" said her grandmother, reaching out to stroke her hair briefly.

"No, it's true," said her mother, as Lyn ducked out from under the hand; being hugged was nice, having your head dabbed at as if you were a dog was not. "They do. They talk about the birds for hours. She's very observant, he says."

"Not very observant about him, though, is she? Come on, Lyn lovey, tell us what he looks like, at least."

Lyn pictured Bill, tall, quite thickset, bulky in sweaters and anorak and heavy corduroy trousers. He seemed indescribable to her. "Oh, I don't know," she said.

"You can tell him from me," said her grandmother playfully, "that I *don't* think you're very observant. I don't think you notice very much at all."

I've noticed him, Lyn thought, I just can't describe him. I've noticed that you've put away Mum and Dad's wedding photo, too, and the one of the three of us – there's only one photo of her and me now – but I can't say it so you'll think I haven't noticed that, either.

"Not to worry," said her grandmother comfortably, "I expect we'll meet him ourselves one of these days."

In the car on the way back to the coast, Lyn said, "Are they coming to visit us down here?"

"No. In spite of what Grandpop says about public transport, it isn't an easy trip without a car."

"Why does Grandma expect to meet Bill, then?"

Her mother was, at that moment, negotiating a roundabout so Lyn didn't expect an immediate answer. "Oh, I don't think she thought it out," she said when they were on the straight again. "I think she somehow always expects to meet people she's heard about."

"Will it be too late to go out with Bill when we get back?"

"Yes. It'll be dusk."

"Oh well. That's all right. I can go first thing tomorrow."

They entered the motorway and travelled a short stretch of it in silence. Then, "Lyn."

"Yes."

"Do you still miss London a lot?"

Lyn considered the question as they left the motorway

and meandered towards the coast road by slower, narrower ways.

"Not at this moment," she said. "It was nice to see traffic again today – see a busy place. I like to think it's all still going on somewhere. But when I'm on the beach I don't miss it." She thought for a bit longer. "I miss Sue," she said, then. "I'd like it if she was up here."

"The people in our new flat," said her mother, "are ringing Grandpop tonight to tell him if they've exchanged contracts. I'm going to ring him from the village tomorrow – so we'll know then when we can move in. If it turns out there's going to be a long delay, you can have Sue to stay here, for part of the Easter holidays. She'd have to bring a sleeping bag and share your room, but you wouldn't mind that, would you?"

"Thanks," said Lyn. "No, that'd be OK."

She conjured up an image of Sue. Great to share a room and talk after they'd gone to bed, great to show her around and explain the dunes and the cliffs and the castle, great to show Bill off to her. But. There was definitely a 'but'. She leant her head against the side window of the car and watched in the wing mirror as the road ran away fast behind them. It was nearly lighting-up time, the cars of the cautious were already aglow with side lights. As she watched, the cars thinned out until theirs was the only one on their bit of road, the bit that would run through the village any moment now and then wind on and turn suddenly left to travel beside the sea. Not many people came this way, it was special and secret, you had to belong to be allowed to come this way. It would be all right for Sue to belong, to be initiated as a special member; that wasn't the 'but'. She tried, she tried hard, but she couldn't work out what the 'but' was. It had something to do with not being quite sure that she wanted Bill to explain about Uncommon Common Gulls and Brown-Headed Black-Headed Gulls to Sue – which he inevitably would do if she was there, because he was a friendly sort of person, and everyone liked Sue. And suppose Sue found the Royal Tern.

They were on the coast road now, driving past the Parkers' house. There was a noticeable greyness about the air, the dunes looked dingy and secretive, like great shoulders hunched under blankets and ready for sleep. The sea had merged with the sky as though a horizon was a day-time convention that could be cast off at bedtime like clothes. There was a light in the Parkers' sitting room and the curtains were still open. Lyn tried to see in as they passed, see if they were all three in there and what they were doing – but though they were not going fast, it was too fast for that, and all she saw was a blur.

The Royal Tern; perhaps that was the 'but'. She couldn't tell Sue about it because she had promised not to tell anyone. Yet it was unthinkable to have a secret from Sue if they were both in the same place – and, what was more, in the same place as the secret itself.

The car crunched on to its gritty parking place and stopped. Lyn climbed out at once and stood in the dying light sniffing the now-familiar thin, salty smell. She knew that Mr Parker could have been mistaken about the bird – yet she didn't believe for one moment that he had been. Nor, she was sure, did Bill. Therefore. Out there on the dim sea a rare bird was dozing, dreaming – did they dream? – of a fishy breakfast.

She followed her mother inside and noted with satisfaction that as soon as she had switched on the side lamps she went to the little grate, where the wood lay waiting.

"Sue can come and stay when we're in the new flat," she said.

"She can certainly do that," said her mother. "But we'll try and get her up here first, I promise. We'll just have to see how the timing goes."

"Yes," said Lyn, thinking that maybe Sue wouldn't be able to come anyway. Then she pushed the whole thing out of her mind because she found it unsettling. Never before, never, had she not wanted to see Sue.

Chapter Fourteen

It was low tide, so after a while they left the road and walked part way around the base of the Castle cliffs – Mr Parker, Buster, Lyn and Bill. From time to time three pairs of binoculars were trained out to sea, although the Terns had found a fishing ground that was pretty well out of sight.

"If you were as dedicated as you ought to be," said Mr Parker to Bill, "you'd be down in one of those natural hides from dawn to dusk."

"And you'd find my skeletal remains in the summer, I suppose."

"We could bring you sandwiches," said Lyn.

"Thanks very much. Why me?"

"I'm too old," said Mr Parker.

"Rubbish."

"We could work out a roster," said Lyn. "Change the watch every three hours or something."

"Don't worry," said Bill easily, "we'll see it. I put in more time than I'm given credit for."

"That's true," said Mr Parker.

"And we're watching now," said Lyn.

"We are," said Mr Parker, "but this doesn't really count. This is not true bird-watching. A true bird-watcher is *never* accompanied by a large dog."

"He wouldn't chase them, would he?"

"No, he wouldn't do that. But he does stagger about in a manner a bird could take to be threatening. And he does snort and gasp, rather, from time to time."

"Not discreet," said Lyn.

"Not discreet," agreed Mr Parker. "I think we might

pause for a bit here. Buster needs a rest." Buster was in fact still plodding onwards, rocking even more than usual as his old pads encountered the low rocky outcrops at the foot of the cliffs, which stretched like roots towards the sea's edge. But no one argued. They sat on rocks of slightly varying heights, their backs against the hard cliff face, and Buster, noticing this, stopped his steady onward plod and began to blow noisily into a nearby rock pool instead.

"Fulmars," said Bill, pointing without lowering the binoculars. "See?"

"Got them," said Lyn, after a brief struggle with her heavy, leather-bound pair. There were only a few, wheeling far out over the sea, only slightly bigger than the Common Gulls but somehow more solid-looking.

"They nest farther along the coast," he said, "where the cliffs are higher."

"When I was considerably younger," said Mr Parker, training his binoculars in the same direction, "I used to climb on those cliffs in spring for a closer look. Very hazardous."

"High?" said Lyn.

"Yes, but it wasn't only that. The Fulmars keep a special greeting for unwanted visitors and if they take you by surprise with it you can easily miss your footing."

"They're the ones," said Bill," – have you heard this, Lyn? – who spit in your eye if you get too close to their nests."

"How disgusting," said Lyn.

"It really is," said Mr Parker, in the complacent tones of one who knows he'll never again be subjected to such an assault. "They regurgitate a really foul, fishy-smelling muck, especially for the purpose. I've been 'got' more than once, I can tell you."

Buster inhaled something unexpected from his rock pool and blew it out again with some force.

"Buster could challenge them to a duel," said Lyn.

"A gobbing contest," said Bill. "Buster versus the Fulmars. Championship stuff."

"Now don't give the girl ideas like that," said Mr Parker. "Her mother'll decide we're not fit company for her."

"How do you feel about stuffed parrots?" said Lyn suddenly.

"They don't spit," said Bill.

"They don't really do much, I suppose," said Mr Parker, patting his knee invitingly until the old dog plodded over and sat on his foot. "Why do you ask?"

"My grandma had a parrot and when it died she had it stuffed," said Lyn. "I can't decide if that was a good idea or not."

Mr Parker leant stiffly forward and enclosed Buster's silky ears in his cupped hands. "Don't let him hear," he said. "He'll have nightmares."

"Sorry, Buster," said Lyn.

"I don't know what I think about it, either," said Bill. "Is it a good-looking parrot?"

"Oh yes. Bright red and blue."

"That's something. But if you've been used to it being alive it must be a sad sight now. You'd constantly be reminded that it can't talk any more."

"It never did talk."

"Ah," said Bill.

"If your grandmother took up ventriloquism," said Mr Parker, "it could start now."

"Speaking of starting," said Bill, "do you think we ought to turn back? It's not really warm enough to sit here for long."

"Buster hasn't had much of a rest," said Mr Parker. "He's only just stopped pottering around."

"It wasn't Buster that wanted the rest," said Bill.

"You could at least humour me," said Mr Parker, getting up from his rock and dusting himself down. "Back we go, then."

"I don't think I really want to go and live near Grandma and Grandpop," said Lyn, half over her shoulder to Bill, as they worked their way back across the rocks in single file. "It was nice going to visit them, but I think I want to live here."

Bill grunted. "Not very adaptable, are you?" he said, as rocks became sand and they scuffed their way in Mr Parker's wake towards the road and easier walking.

"Yes, very," said Lyn indignantly. "I think I've adapted very fast."

"You'll adapt fast again, then, won't you? It goes on all through life, you know, this adapting lark."

"I wonder how Sharon's doing," said Lyn vaguely, stopping at the edge of the road to empty some sand out of her shoe. She couldn't pull it off without unlacing it, so she had to sit down and attend to it properly.

"Worked out every possible route home and unsticking lifts daily, I expect."

Lyn stared up at him from her seat on the sandy tarmac. "I didn't think you were listening when I told you all that," she said. She retied her shoe and Bill held out his hands to her and pulled her to her feet again. "I always listen," he said. "Rude not to."

"You wouldn't like it here in the winter," said Mr Parker, over his shoulder, leading the way with Buster beside him. "Very bleak."

"I like bleak places," said Lyn.

"I thought you liked noise and crowds and urban life," said Bill.

"They have their place," said Lyn. "Don't laugh at me."

"No," said Mr Parker, "don't laugh at her. Buster and I don't like being laughed at, either."

"Any chance of bird-watching near your new flat?" said Bill.

"Mum says my room looks out over allotments and the railway line," said Lyn. "Any good?"

"Should be very good," said Bill. "Didn't you look out?"

"Oh, we didn't go there. I'm glad really. The other people are still in it and I wouldn't want to see it for the first time with – usurpers – in it."

"Strictly," said Bill, "I think you're the usurpers."

"No," said Lyn, "they want to go. We're just taking over. We're usurpers in this cottage, though. You normally stay there, don't you?"

"I do usually."

"Do you think of us as usurpers?"

"No," said Bill, as they drew level with the Parkers' house. "Holiday cottages are like library books, you can't expect to own them."

"Coming in for a spot of lunch?" said Mr Parker to Bill.

"Yes, thanks. Even though I shall be accused of abandoning the watch."

Mr Parker chuckled. "See you later, Lyn," he said, as the three of them turned in at the gate.

Lyn waved and wandered on home for her own lunch.

"Two weeks," said her mother, as she closed the door behind her.

"What?"

"Two weeks! We can move in two weeks. We've got a firm date. So I suggest you write to Sue and see if her mother will let her come up for a few days. Would she travel alone on the train, do you know, if we meet her at the station?"

"She always goes alone when she visits her dad," said Lyn.

"That's all right, then."

It turned out that there was plenty of time in which to word a letter to Sue because, during lunch, a fine misting rain began to fall, and by the time the dishes were cleared it was quite heavy.

"I've got an anorak," said Lyn. "I won't melt away in a bit of rain."

"Your shoes'll get wet and so will your jeans. I don't want you down with a cold."

"Bill will be out there, you can bet."

"When you're as old as Bill, you can do as you like."

"Not if you're still my mother, I won't be able to."

Her mother looked cross for a moment, and then laughed. "Behave, or I'll set Grandpop on you," she said.

"Oh no," said Lyn, clutching at her throat. "Anything but that."

"You've been out for hours and hours today already. Just settle down quietly for a bit. It may clear later."

It didn't. The rain fell steadily and quite quietly. There was no wind to blow it away and no sign of the clouds emptying themselves. Lyn was not as put out as she might have been because she was struggling with her letter to Sue, and it filled up a surprising amount of time. The part where she told her about the visit to her grandparents was all right, it was the invitation that kept coming out all wrong. Each time she read the page through she found that some phrase like, "if you really want to", or "if you haven't anything better to do", or "not that there's anything much up here", had crept in, and she had to rewrite the whole thing in order to leave it out. She had finally admitted to herself what the 'but' was. She wanted Bill to herself, she didn't want to share him with Sue. But there was no doubt that Sue would enjoy it up here, and she had decided not to be mean.

She was aware of her mother moving around the little house as she struggled – clearing out and relaying the fire, having a nice-smelling bath in the lean-to bathroom behind the kitchen, moving in the kitchen itself – but she didn't bother to look round. She just stared from time to time across the little table to the rain spotted window, and then returned to the letter. She had just finished it, and licked and sealed its envelope, when her mother put a mat, knife, fork and spoon by her elbow and said, "Lay your place for tea, will you?"

Lyn moved the cardboard writing box and the finished letter to the side table by the armchair that she regarded as hers. She had just set her place when her mother reappeared beside her and put a plate on the mat; a hot plate with fish fingers, baked beans and a potato on it. Lyn was surprised. This was about twenty minutes earlier than usual.

"Aren't you having any?" she said, sitting down to it, noticing that no other place was laid at the table.

"No, I'm eating later." She went in to the tiny kitchen to fetch the ketchup and set it on the table by Lyn's plate. "The Parkers are coming over soon."

Lyn looked at her for the first time since lunch. She was all dressed up, wearing her flowery dress with the black belt, the one she hardly ever wore – now – and her black shoes with the thin heels. A party, thought Lyn, pleased, swallowing her mouthful of beans, and surely if the Parkers were coming over their lodger would come too. She decided to wear her red dress, the one with the white collar – as long as they'd brought it with them and not put it in store; she couldn't remember.

Then she realised something was not quite right. "The Parkers are coming here to eat?" she said warily. "Couldn't I have waited to eat with you?"

"No, they're coming to babysit."

Lyn let go of her knife and fork. "What?"

Her mother sat down at the table opposite her, leaning her elbows on the empty space where her own fish fingers should have been.

"I'm sorry," she said. "That's a really silly expression. I don't mean you're a baby, but I wouldn't leave you in the house on your own. I don't mean to be like Grandpop, I know you'd be fine, but I just wouldn't be happy about it."

"But where will you be?" said Lyn, a horrid possibility coming to her.

Her mother smiled. She had lipstick on. She hardly ever

wore lipstick. She gave a little half-shrug, almost as if she was embarrassed. "Bill and I are going out for a meal. He knows a nice inn. It's only about fifteen miles from here. We won't be late."

Lyn stared at her in blank amazement, and words churned around her head so fast that they all got wedged together and none of them would come out. "He won't like those silly shoes," she wanted to say, "he likes sneakers, that you can walk on sand dunes in." Or, "He won't like that scent, he likes that cold salty smell." Or, "You can't make him go to an inn, he doesn't like inns, he likes the beach."

She pushed her plate hard away from her, so that its rim banged into the wall, half hoping it would crack, which it didn't, and screamed across at her mother, "You can't! You can't DO that! He's my friend. He's MY friend!"

Chapter Fifteen

In the morning, immediately after breakfast, Lyn wandered out on to the dunes on her own. To her surprise and irritation, she had slept through her mother's return and the Parkers' departure. At breakfast she had asked no questions about the evening, and her mother had volunteered no information. Neither of them mentioned the row they had had. They were polite to each other but withdrawn. It was as if neither of them was really present in her own body.

The sun was out, though the breeze was chilly, and the dune sand sparkled a welcome. "Hang on in there, Marram Grass," Lyn whispered through slightly chattering teeth. "I'm coming up."

She ran quickly to the crest of the dune system, setting her feet sideways the way she had noticed that Bill did. At the top she screwed up her eyes and looked out towards the sea. The Terns were further in than yesterday, most of them bobbing in the shallows but a few standing about on shore. Thinking about nests, she supposed. They stood around in an exclusive group, away from the Ringed Plovers and from the ever-busy Turnstones, which she could only recognise from where she stood by their distinctive movements.

She felt as though she had lost something, which would in some curious way be returned to her if she could only find the Royal Tern. "Let me be the one to see it," she kept repeating in her mind, although she didn't know who she was asking. She didn't feel that a prayer, about something which should be so unimportant, would be appropriate. She began to believe she was asking the bird itself.

There were definitely more Terns today than there had

been yesterday. She slithered down the scratchy sliding sand into one of the natural hides and lay on her stomach in it, resting her chin on her crossed arms. For once she didn't hope to see Bill, in fact she was relieved that there was no sign of him. She thought she would like to stay where she was for the rest of the day – but she knew that they would only come looking for her and that she would not be hard to find. It was only the birds who chose to believe the dunes were empty of all human life if you simply ducked down out of sight for a while.

There was no sense of time down on the beach. If anyone in London had told her that one day she would spend an hour, maybe two hours, maybe more, quite still, just watching birds lead their lives, she would have said they were daft, but, unless the sun actually began to set, there was really nothing to indicate that so much time was drifting by. Even the tide, visibly creeping in, or gently pulling back leaving its rim of wet sand and bits of weed stuck with feathers, didn't seem to relate to time. It was like being in a separate compartment in the world, where time as a dimension did not exist. It was sometimes quite shocking to rejoin the rest of the world and find that time had been rushing by in her absence.

Lyn gazed dreamily across at the activity on the shore and in the shallows, and wondered how she could ever have thought there was only one kind of white screaming gull. The Ringed Plovers and Turnstones weren't even white, and the rest were so different from one another, different in size, different in the colour of their accessories – legs, beaks and heads mostly – that she couldn't understand how she had ever mixed them up.

Then, remembering Mr Parker's notebooks, she decided she should really count the Terns. Not that she had brought her own notebook with her, but then one number shouldn't be too hard to remember. She lay there, feeling the sand shift and then settle hard and firm beneath her, and nar-

rowed her eyes to try and count the short-legged streamlined white birds with the little flat wings. It wasn't easy.
One would fly and return to a different place. One would
masquerade as a Common Gull. A Common Gull in flight
would masquerade as a Tern. This place is getting
unreasonable again, she thought. Everything's going to
come to pieces. The sand slid softly and secretly into her
right shoe. The Terns flew about, bobbed about, strutted
about. Two of them had a brief squabble when they both
wanted to stand on the same bit of sand.

Bully! thought Lyn, scowling at the one who had seemed
to her to be the aggressor. Just because you've been doing
your weight-training and got yourself a bit bigger than the
others.

She realised the significance of what she was thinking
and cupped her hands around her eyes to try to focus better
on the one bird. In her hurry to get out of the house that
morning she had not only forgotten her notebook, she had
forgotten her gift binoculars as well.

One of the Terns did seem bigger than the rest, did look
slightly different. But it was too far away, and the sea
behind it was reflecting too much of a glare, and it was too
busy moving around for her to get a good look.

Now she did want Bill. Bill and his binoculars. Or Mr
Parker and his. The Royal Tern just might be down there on
the beach, and here she was, perhaps actually looking at it,
but unable to be sure. Oh BE the right one, she said to it in
her mind, it wouldn't hurt you to be the right one.

She stood up and looked around. Emptiness. It was not
like the emptiness she thought she had seen when she first
arrived, because it had a pattern now, and inhabitants she
knew by sight, even if most of them wore feathers. But it
seemed wholly empty of human life.

She had a terrible sense of urgency and didn't know what
to do with it. She could search the dune system for Bill,
which might take ages. She could go to the Parkers' house

on the unlikely chance that Bill would be there and, even if he wasn't, at least enlist Mr Parker's help. Or she could go home for her binoculars.

She decided she didn't want to seek Bill out and say, "It might be there, come and look." Then he would be the one to identify it. In fact he might even be watching it from somewhere at this moment. Much better to be able to say to him, "It's there and I've seen it." That way, even if he had seen it too, he would have to give her credit for recognising it herself.

She set off rapidly for home, completely forgetting that she had wanted to stay away for hours. Home was nearest, and it was binoculars she needed first – not Bill or Mr Parker, not yet.

She hurried across the road, opened the front door and went into the sitting room, intending to run straight for the stairs and her bedroom, where the binoculars stood importantly on her bedside table.

But in the sitting room, sitting at the small table and each holding a mug of coffee, sat her mother and Bill. They were laughing together about something that had been said before she had opened the door.

Lyn stopped so suddenly that she stumbled and almost fell. They hadn't called her, hadn't said, "We're having coffee, do you want anything?" Hadn't thought about her at all. She and the Royal Tern had been out on the beach together and here they sat, laughing about something – what was there to laugh about . . .

They both looked round as she exploded into the room, both turned their smiling faces to her, both said, "Hallo."

Lyn ignored them, crossed the room quickly and ran up the stairs, hitting them as hard with her feet as she could. She went in to her bedroom and picked up the binoculars.

All that time they'd spent together – last evening and now this morning – obviously he must have told her about the Tern by now. There was a limit, Lyn thought, to what

they could talk about without mentioning it, since it was the
whole point and purpose of his visit here. How silly, how
sad, how awful, there they were talking about it, won-
dering about it, and all they had to do was go outside –
unless, of course, she was mistaken.

She walked out of her bedroom and shut the door as
loudly as she could. She could feel the sound reverberate all
over the little house. She almost expected to hear things fall
over and break, but nothing did. She ran down the stairs
again, as heavily as her lightweight and sandy sneakers
would allow.

"Lyn, come and join us," said her mother, too brightly,
too cheerfully, too obviously ignoring the slammed door.
"Would you like some milk and a biscuit?"

Too late, Lyn thought grimly. She said nothing to them,
didn't even look at them, crossed the room, went out of the
front door and then – for maximum effect – closed it behind
her so quietly that even she barely heard the click.

She hurried across the road, not allowing herself to turn
to see if they were looking after her out of the window.
Because of course they wouldn't be, they'd be far too busy
talking their secret talk, laughing their secret laughs.

Back among the sand dunes she wriggled herself into
position, propped herself on her elbows and carefully
focused the glasses. She half expected to find that the birds
had moved off along the beach and that this was no longer
the right place to be. But they were still there, in amongst
the rest.

If it is, if I'm right, I'll tell Mr Parker, she thought. No
one else. NO ONE else.

She moved the glasses, slowly, carefully, remembering
Mr Parker's words over tea and crumpets days ago – "It's
wise to remember that if you think you've glimpsed something extraordinarily rare, you're almost certainly mistaken." Almost certainly. But . . .

Among the Sandwich Terns, the white bird walked. Like

them, but different, bigger, and with a vivid red bill that would have marked it out, even if nothing else had, from the rest. A Royal Tern, against all likelihood, alive and well and hundreds and thousands of miles away from home.

When Lyn stood up she didn't know what she was going to do. Even when she began to run, she didn't really know what she was doing. She ran from the shifting dune sand down on to the hard compacted sand below, and went on running, towards the sea, towards the birds, the binoculars beating at her rib cage with every step as though, in their age and wisdom, they were trying to make her stop. At her approach the birds began to rise, not just the Terns but all of them, wheeling in panic, and as they rose and screamed so Lyn began to scream, too, waving her arms and shrieking like the gulls, running, waving, yelling, right into the shallows, kicking up spray, until she'd emptied the beach and filled the sky with crying, feathered chaos.

Some of them, braver or more aggressive, stayed nearby, not landing, cruising, glaring at her out of one eye and then the other. Some settled way out to sea where they bobbed resentfully on the wave crests, scattered, no longer in their comfortable groups. The Terns went far out to sea, way out, beyond the vale of hazy light that was reflecting from it, out of sight; all of them. No Sandwich Terns. No Royal Tern. All gone.

Lyn stood with the cruelly cold water up to her ankles, her sodden shoes feeling heavy even though she was standing still, and thought for a moment that a fog was coming down over the sea – then realised that she was crying.

She turned, still in the sea, to see a tall figure walking rapidly across the beach towards her, dark against the pale sand. Bill had followed her out of the house, must have seen what she had done, was coming now to meet her.

She stood where she was and felt as though she was shrivelling in front of him into something small and ugly and repulsive. There was no reason to give, no excuse to offer, you couldn't even say sorry for something so awful, so cruelly destructive.

Bill bore down on her, his face seeming quite blank, then when he was almost in the water himself he shot out a long arm and caught her by the wrist. Lyn pulled back, but he drew her firmly out of the water and on to the wet sand at its edge. Then he squatted down in front of her and shook her very slightly. "I'm sorry," he said. "We didn't mean to hurt you."

He didn't have his huge anorak on, just his brown cords and dingy brown sweater, but he still had a pocket, in his trousers, and from this he produced a handkerchief and began to mop and wipe at her wet face rather as if he was cleaning the windscreen of a car. "We didn't mean to shut you out," he said. "Honestly."

"You don't . . . " Lyn began, then had a coughing fit. "You don't know what I did," she said, when she could.

"Yes, I do. You took it out on the birds," said Bill, launching into another mopping session, since more had appeared to be mopped. "You've given them all hysterics and the vapours and they've gone away to sulk."

"But I'm so stupid," said Lyn.

"We're all stupid. It's the human condition."

"But I *saw* it," Lyn wailed, now wanting to shake him into understanding the enormity of her crime. It was intolerable to think he was forgiving her without realising the full awfulness of what she had done. "I saw the Royal Tern."

But, "I guessed you had," said Bill, shifting his crouching weight a little. "It was the final blow, wasn't it?"

Lyn stared at him, unable to understand why he bothered to talk to her at all.

"Now are you sure?" he said, calmly but very seriously. "Are you absolutely certain?"

She watched him and swallowed a few times. "Yes," she said. "I am sure, I am quite certain."

"Excellent. Mr Parker is vindicated."

"But it's gone," said Lyn. "I chased it away. It's lost. It's millions of miles from its home and it had just found a new place and settled and made friends and now I've spoiled everything for it and it's lost again and alone . . ."

Bill shrugged. "I expect it's mucking about with the Sandwich Terns," he said, "out there somewhere. In three thousand miles of Atlantic Ocean, it'll have seen worse things than you. It'll probably come back to this beach later on. Tomorrow maybe . . ."

"But if they'd been nesting . . ." She had a hazy image of a bald baby bird, abandoned to starvation by its parents.

"That would have been more serious."

"I might have done it when they were nesting." She had an image of a bald baby half-brother, manoeuvred into danger.

"But you didn't."

"I might have."

"I might have fallen out of a tree when I was seven and broken my neck and then I wouldn't be here at all."

"But I really might have."

"And I really might have. I used to climb far too high. What are you after? Do you want me to be angry with you?"

"No."

"That's a relief. Lyn, you can have all sorts of different friends in life, you know. Because we've become friends, that doesn't mean you and Sue aren't friends any more. And because I'm friendly with your mother doesn't mean I'm not your friend, too."

A movement on the dunes caught Lyn's eye. "She's there," she said.

Bill stood up. "Come on," he said, and began to walk up the beach. Lyn took the handkerchief from his hand and blew her nose, twice, then walked with him, her shoes making appalling noises as her feet expelled water from them with every step.

"What's happening?" said her mother, as they reached her. She didn't have a coat or jacket on, either, and she had her arms wrapped around herself as if that would keep out the cold.

"Terrific news!" said Bill. "Lyn has just confirmed a sighting of an extremely rare bird. That's why she rushed through. She needed her binoculars urgently."

"Are you teasing me?"

"Certainly not. You saw it, didn't you, Lyn?"

"Yes," said Lyn quietly. "A Royal Tern."

"A what!" said her mother.

"Didn't you know it might be here?" said Lyn. "Didn't Bill tell you about it? It's why he's here."

Her mother looked from one to the other of them. "No," she said blankly. "I didn't know. A Royal what? And Lyn, why are you crying?"

Lyn, standing more or less between them, half trying to listen through the back of her head to the shore behind her, willing the birds confused shrieks to return to normal, couldn't think of an answer.

But Bill brushed the question easily aside. "Oh, don't worry about that," he said. "The first sighting of a really rare bird is always an emotional experience."

He glanced over his shoulder, screwing his eyes up against the glare, and looked rather hopefully along the beach.

Lyn, who couldn't bring herself to look around, watched his face, but he didn't seem to see anything worth looking at and turned back again. He shrugged, perhaps with the cold, and rubbed his hands together. "Let's all go inside," he said, "it's parky out here."

THE HORN OF MORTAL DANGER

Lawrence Leonard

When Jen and her brother Widgie stumble across a secret underground world, they find themselves in the middle of a war between two rival factions, the Railwaymen and Canal Folk. It is the start of a thrilling and dangerous adventure.

"A fantasy whose words are forcefully visual, whose concept is original and compelling."
Growing Point

"A lively, original and exciting adventure story."
The Times Literary Supplement

THE TIME TREE
Enid Richemont

Rachel and Joanna are best friends and the tall tree in the park is their special place. It's Anne's too. So it hardly seems surprising that the three girls meet up there – except for the fact that four centuries divide their lives.

"Ms Richemont develops her story beautifully, with finely controlled writing and clear delineation of her three main characters."
The Junior Bookshelf